THE FINGER OF GOD

THE FINGER OF GOD

JEFF MALPHURS

For Angie,
Together, we've lived a better story
than any I could ever write.

Chapter 1

I was on a train. Not in the passenger car or anything fancy like that. Not on top, like a white-hat cowboy chasing a bad guy with a swirly mustache. Not in a box car either. To be sure, I don't hop on trains like a vagabond. No, I was on the front of the engine, hanging onto the tippy-top of the metal cow-catching grill deal.

How I got there, I can't say. Who can explain dreams or why we do what we do within them? I just know I was traveling down that track fast. Might as well have been a bullet train for the speed I was going. I never actually saw the length of the train snaking behind me. I was looking out in front of it. I knew I was on it, though, going lickety split down those tracks, passing pine trees and palmettos, the wooden ties rocketing past my feet. I couldn't hear the engine either. Just the wind. Oh, the wind in my ears was loud. I couldn't hear anything else but that cruel, relentless wind. That is, until the train whistle sounded right behind me. If I ever doubted I was on a train, that assured me I was.

At some point, I veered off the tracks, and for a second, I thought I was derailing. Gonna be one of those dreams, I thought. Some people dream of crossing a bridge and it grows too steep and they fall backwards off of it. Some dream the bridge collapses and they fall from it that way. But I grew up and lived my whole life a short ways from the railroad tracks, so it made sense that I dreamed of trains derailing and blasting through my living room.

That didn't happen, though. In this dream, with me on the front of the train, I never even saw my house. Instead, I sped over our neighborhood's crossing and right toward the lone oak tree that stood in the grassy field a stone's throw from my front door. I recognized it right away. Had I looked around, I suppose I would have seen my house over my left shoulder. Would've seen the tracks over my right for that matter. But I didn't. I just stared at the tree, finding something interesting about it and its broad, sweeping canopy for the first time in my life. Like the train tracks, the oak had always been there.

The wind whipped through her branches, causing her leaves to nearly give way in the gale. Then, just like that, the wind died to an easy breeze. I circled the tree then, knowing full well I wasn't on the train anymore. I was floating over and around her outstretched limbs, caught adrift like a feather in the now gentle wisp.

In this dream, something about that tree held my interest. In my waking hours, I never paid trees too much mind. I looked at it as I floated around it. Inspected it. I totally expected to see something in it and I prepared myself for the thing that would jolt me awake. Maybe the wind would die to nothing and I'd fall flat on my face or a branch would give way and come at me. Or red eyes would shoot open in the darkness of the canopy and stare at me, dreadful fangs beneath them. Dreams often have a jarring moment, don't they? That flash before you that ends your sleep in an instant and has you gasping, wondering if you heard a door slam or a person scream.

But nothing like that happened. I lifted from my slumber, slow and easy, as the tree faded from my vision and the light of dawn reached its pink tendrils through my bedside window blinds. My last glimpse of the tree gave me something, though. Just a fleeting look. I'll never know if it was part of my dream or a suggestion of my waking mind. Beneath her canopy, I saw a shadow. Or better yet, a silhouette of a tall, rail-thin man leaning against her wide trunk. In the instant I noticed it, the ghostly image faded to nothingness, and I opened my eyes.

I awoke, as I did every morning, to the sound of the 6am train blowing its whistle as it went over the crossing an eighth of a mile from my house. I left my strange dream behind, floating somewhere in the ether between alertness and the Sandman's realm. Had I tried harder to remember it or take note of it, I would have known what I had experienced wasn't a dream. It wasn't even a nightmare.

It was a warning.

Chapter 2

Doreen Street. My street. I loved it in the mid-morning. I know I said I woke up at dawn, but I didn't really get moving until a few hours later. That happens with age. I used to be eager to tackle the day. Now, I'm happy to let it amble up to me in its own time. Maybe I'll jump on its back and take a ride. Maybe I'll let it keep going on by and I'll just hang back and watch it find its way to others with a more motivated mindset.

My street cut right down the middle of a working-class neighborhood with modest bungalow-style homes on each side. Power poles lined it like lights on a runway. Near the tracks, opposite the field with that big oak tree from my dream, was a community playground. I could see it all from my house. I didn't have a porch. Just an elevated entryway to my front door. My little house had a pretty big crawlspace, which let the air get under it and helped keep it cool in the Florida heat. And, Lord, it was already hot.

Since my raised entryway didn't have room for a chair, I sat on the top step and looked out over the neighborhood. The little awning over the porch steps offered some shade from the sun, so I didn't mind sitting there with my coffee and watching the neighborhood come alive.

Fridays in the summer were easy days. Lay low days. Right up my alley.

A group of young children were already playing in the park. Three of them. Loud little rascals too, but there are worse sounds in the world than kids having fun. Their momma sat on a bench nearby, nose in her phone.

Past them sauntered that black lab mixed-with-something-else pup from another street. Conrad Lane, I believe. That's where the white folks' area brushed up against ours with the railroad tracks in between. She'd gotten away again and was all too happy to trot down our road, dragging her red leash behind her. I never did see that mongrel without her leash. When I said it was red, I meant it used to be red a few weeks before. It hadn't taken it long for the sun to turn it pink. The pavement had darn near worn down the loop handle to threads over that time, too. Never saw anyone come looking for her. I always flipped her a cookie if she came near me. I didn't mind sharing my breakfast with Daizy Mae. That's what I called her. Never knew her real name.

Down the road a bit, the neighbors were getting into their morning chores. There was Agnes, watering the plants on her front porch. She had a nice porch. Plenty of room for a chair. She always said hose water only kept her plants alive, but they needed rain to grow. She sure loved those plants. Spindly things if you ask me. Every turn of the season, she'd go to the nursery and get some new ones to put in her big pots. Every season, the heat would drain them of life, rain or no rain. See, the problem was, she would get plants that looked pretty in the store but weren't meant for our area. They were pretty elsewhere. Just not meant for us. That was life on Doreen Street, though. A lot of things weren't meant for us. But what do I know about gardening?

Next door to her was Manny, a chubby guy in his late twenties. He didn't do much during the day, but he came alive at night. Was up at all hours, riding around in his car, doing God knows what. Didn't have no job that I could tell. Not my business though, as he was sure to tell me on more than one occasion. Manny was washing his car in his driveway. Like Agnes with her plants, he took great pride in his car. It was a nice car. One of those fast and loud Dodge Chargers. Not the old, good-looking ones like from the 70s, though. It was new, within a few years, and he had souped it up big-time. Loud radio with big speakers in the back that ate up all his trunk space and shook the windows of every house within a mile. Dark windows. Rims like I'd never seen. They were the kind that kept spinning somehow when the tires stopped. Lights on the undercarriage. Now what in the world are the use of lights that run along the bottom of a car? Anyway, that car was nice and was one of those things probably not meant for our area either. Manny, with no job, managed to work it out. Not speculating how, but I can say one thing. I never really liked Manny much.

Daizy Mae ran up to Manny about then. Maybe she just wanted a drink from his hose, but he shooed her off. What bother would it have been to give that poor ol' girl a drink, this heat being like it was? That was Manny. Daizy Mae turned around and came back toward me, dragging that sun-bleached leash. She was a curious, precocious girl. Always friendly. Good thing I saved her a cookie, hard as it was not to eat it myself. I turned on my hose and she drank from the spout. Must have appreciated it, because she loved on me a good while after that.

When she was done, she trotted back in the direction from where she had come, toward the playground and the tracks. Which meant she went in front of Joe Moore's house, but not before going by his daughter's. Felicia's house was right smack between mine and Joe's.

I got up and followed her path. Felicia's house was quiet. She never had a proper driveway. Her car was always in a different spot in her front yard. She didn't have much in the way of grass, so I guess it didn't matter where she parked. Although, I figured she didn't have grass on account of her haphazard park jobs. I could always tell how much of a hurry she was in by how close to the front door her car was. Lately, she'd taken a shine to parking right at the base of the big power pole that was on the corner of her lot and her dad's. It didn't make any difference to me where she parked her car, but she was so close to that pole that it would've been hard to get in the passenger's side door. Just didn't make good sense to me to park there.

Joe's house was the onliest place I liked better than my own. And one good reason for that was playing in a sandbox me and Joe had built in the front yard by his porch. Little Willie was three and playing away in the box. What a sweet boy. Just an absolute joy to watch, I can tell you. He had a megawatt smile that could light up the outside in the dead of night. Sweet boy, he was.

His granddaddy, Joe, was right on the porch, overseeing him. Joe was a couple of years younger than me. Sixty-eight at his last birthday. He was short, no more than 5'6". Since I was darn near a foot taller (not quite, maybe, but a respectable 6'3"), I could look right down on the top of his head, and often did, just to rile him up. Joe always dressed in ragged blue jeans and that threadbare white, button-up shirt of his. Most times, he was barefoot.

Well, that boy had come by his smile honestly, because Joe had a big one. It wasn't as readily available as it used to be, nor was it as often an occurrence as Willie's, but when it was there, it was still worth a million bucks. Willie was just about the only thing that made Joe smile anymore, so I was happy to see Joe smiling when I walked up. Joe was missing a front tooth. He did a good job of hiding it most of the time, but a Willie-induced smile put that empty space on full display.

Joe's porch was big and wide and nicely covered. It even had a ceiling fan that kept that thick, stifling air moving. He rocked easily in one of two rocking chairs by the front door. He didn't even see me walk up since he was so focused on that boy. I was on the first step before he looked at me.

"Hot one today," I said. That's usually how we started our day.

"Swampy," he replied, per usual.

"Don't Felicia got the meeting with the doctors today?" I asked.

"Yep."

Soon as Joe answered, the front door flew open and out came Joe's wife, Yvette. After her came their daughter, Felicia. Yvette was Joe's age but looked a lot younger than him. I think it was all the lotion she put on. Felicia was in her mid-thirties by now, I reckon. They were in a hurry.

"Bye-bye, baby-boy!" Yvette chirped to little Willie as she scrambled down the steps, getting her purse just right on her shoulder. She gave me a smile on her way by, but it wasn't like the ones that grandbaby of hers could bring out. Joe hopped to his feet and followed Felicia, who followed Yvette, down the front steps. I don't think Felicia even saw me.

"Willie, get outta that sand! You just had a bath." Felicia looked back at Joe, following her. She was made-up, dressed nice, and as pretty as a picture, but her stress was hard to miss. She wore it like an ox yoke. "Daddy, he's gonna get filthy."

She didn't wait around to see if Willie listened to her. She dug her keys from her purse and pounded her way to her car. By the middle of Joe's yard, Yvette was following her, and Joe was having trouble keeping up.

Felicia jerked open her car's door, ever in a rush. Ever on edge. Of course, she was going to have to back out from beside the pole for her momma to get in. Knew it.

Joe stood next to her and held the door open while she put on her seatbelt. "Why can't I come with y'all. Doctor Dawkins will give it to me straight."

"Oh, he won't talk straight with me?" She was nearly barking at her poor daddy.

"'Course he will. I didn't mean he wouldn't. I just think that if I--"

"Daddy, quit. Just quit! He isn't going to be the only doctor there, so you won't be able to jabber your nonsense at him. I can't have you blowing up and acting like this is something you can just scare into submission!" Nobody gave it hard to Joe like Felicia did.

"What's that supposed to mean?" Nobody but Felicia got Joe so defensive.

"It means this isn't going to go away just because you say it must!"

She slammed her door, cranked her car, and backed out a bit to clear the pole. Joe hurried around behind the car and opened the passenger's door for Yvette, who got in. Before he closed the door, he stooped down and looked across at Felicia.

"Do I embarrass you that much?" he asked her and I felt immediately bad for him.

"Daddy..." Felicia started, maybe realizing she had been a little rough on him. She didn't say anything more.

"Honey, you're in charge of Willie and that's the most important thing in the world right now," Yvette said, ever the peacekeeper of the trio. "Don't let him exert himself too much." She kissed Joe's cheek, and he stepped back so she could close the door.

Felicia spun the car backwards into the road. Before she rocketed out of sight, Yvette rolled down the window and waved at mostly Willie, and maybe a little bit at me.

"You boys be good now. Stay out of trouble!" Then, off they went.

Joe kept waving goodbye as they went on by the field with the oak tree, over the train tracks, and disappeared from view.

When Joe came back to the porch, after his requisite grin at Willie, I could tell he was at an all-time low. Joe was and had been my best friend for as long as I could remember. Like the railroad tracks and the oak tree, he had always been there. For all that time, he had always had an indomitable spirit.

I hated to see him under the weather.

Chapter 3

We settled into our regular routine before long, each sitting in our favorite chair, rocking slowly, watching Willie play. At least I was. Joe was staring off somewhere else. He didn't feel like talking, which for most of his life was an extreme rarity but had become all too common lately.

"Good Lord, it's hot," I said. I dug my handkerchief from my pocket and mopped my forehead. I wasn't talking just to talk. It was surely hot. "I'm sweating like someone sprayed me with a fire hydrogen." Joe looked sideways at me, but he didn't say anything back. "You'd have thought, at some point in all our years, we'd have learnt to play chess." It was something I said every now and again when I was feeling bored or unaccomplished. Usually Joe agreed, or said we'd do it tomorrow, then we'd go about the business of not learning to play chess. Not that day, though. He didn't so much as grunt a reply, so I cut to the chase of what I figured was bothering him. "Willie's gonna be alright, Joe. Doctor Dawkins will make sure of that. You'll see."

Still, nothing from Joe. He just kept staring at something with a grim face. I finally looked up to see what he was so locked in on. I didn't immediately see.

"Hey, bubba, what do you make of that guy?" He growled the words.

"Where?" I asked, genuinely not seeing who he was talking about.

"There." He slowly raised his arm, finger already extended like the Reaper, and pointed across the street to the field.

I finally saw him. A tall, lanky fellow. He was under the big oak, leaning against its trunk. Under the sweeping canopy's shade, he was nothing but a silhouette. My blood ran cold, finally giving me that startled awake moment that had been missing in my dream.

"Who? That guy?" I said, barely able to get the words out. "He ain't nothing."

"He watching those kids in the park, you think?" Joe shook his head. "I don't like that."

"Come on up here, Willie-boy!" I said, waving that resplendent little man up to me. "Come see me a minute. I ain't got to talk to you none yet."

Willie heard me. He seemed like he had been waiting for me to ask. Up those stairs, he trotted. Then, he climbed in my lap. He rested the back of his head on my chest and we rocked a little faster. I instinctively put my arm around his belly, as if to keep him from falling. It wasn't that, though. It was a protective gesture, and I knew it when I did it.

"You got any coffee?" I said, hoping to pull Joe's eyes from that skinny man under the tree. "Some of that Columbia Bean would sure hit the spot."

"Too hot for that," he said.

"Too early for Ol' Red's too, I suppose," I said.

"Yes. Lord, yes. Way too early." Joe finally broke his stare and glanced at me. "Yvette made some iced tea, though." He pushed himself up from the rocker. "Keep an eye out." He shifted his eyes back to the skinny man, then to me. Maybe that was when he saw my arm around Willie like a shield and knew I was already on guard duty.

Joe went into the house, so I turned my attention to the Stranger's silhouette for a moment. Man or ghost, I couldn't be sure. I felt Willie looking up at me. I tickled him and he gave a giggle. Sweet music to my ears.

We were doing the little piggy thing when Joe came out with two glasses of iced tea.

"And this little piggy went to town," I was saying. Willie was grinning. "And this little wolfie huffed and he puffed and he blew the house down!" I tickled him again and he burst out with a gush of laughter.

Joe gave me a glass and sat back down. "There ain't no big bad wolf in 'This Little Piggy'," he griped.

"Say there ain't? Huh," I said. "I seem to recall there was."

I put Willie down and sipped on my tea. "Yes, sir. Just the way I like it." Willie ambled back down the steps and into the yard.

Joe watched Willie until he was in the sandbox. Then, he found the Stranger once more. So far, he hadn't seemed to have moved a muscle.

"What're we smoking tonight?" I asked.

"Ribs. Got 'em thawing now."

"We best not wait too late to start 'em, 'cuz I hear some weather might be on the way."

That ripped Joe's gaze from the Stranger. He peered at me with a new concern. "How bad?"

"Bad enough you might be in the closest quivering like a skitter skunk while the rest of us is chawing ribs." I said it with a laugh because, to me, it was hilarious.

Joe waved me off. "I can't help that I don't like thunder."

"Grown man who hides from noise! Beats all I ever did see!" It was the rare thing I could really razz Joe about. It had been the one fear I ever knew him to have. He took the joke as it was intended and had always smiled when I poked him about it, kind of like when I pointed out he was short. He knew it was a weird thing to be scared of bad storms at his age, especially since we lived in hurricane central like we did, but he really couldn't do a thing about it. Thunder and lightning mortified him. I took the chance to hopefully turn his mood and he responded like I knew he would. "You know, if Felicia parked her car in one spot, she might grow some grass in her front yard."

"Yesterday you were harping on me about cutting my grass too short saying I was gonna kill it. Today it's that Felicia don't have none. I figure she must park her car on that over-sized punkin-head of yours 'cuz you ain't got a stitch of cover on it."

Did I mention I was as bald as they come? Had been since I was thirty-five.

"If you had something as pretty to behold as my noggin, you wouldn't want to cover it up neither." I rubbed my head, sweaty though it was.

"If that's the case, then why do I wear pants?" Joe grinned as he said it. I just about fell out of my chair from laughing so hard. We sure did cut up.

That good-natured turn was only a glimpse of how we spent most of our days. Most of the time, that's how we carried on. Laughing. Razzing each other. Falling out. He was quick-witted. More so than me, so he usually had me in stitches. I wish we would have stayed like that longer that day, so we could have acted the fool like we used to, but things had been different lately. Understandably so. I still missed those old times, though. And our little revisit was over as quick as it started because Joe looked back at the Stranger. His mood darkened again as he nudged me with his elbow.

"He's moving."

The Stranger came out from under the tree and started walking toward the street. He was a tall, skinny, white man, and he wore a tattered blazer and loose, grimy trousers. Like Joe, he was barefoot, but his feet were so dirty they were nearly black. His hair was messy and wind-blown. He was sweating profusely. I'm talking a lot. Even for the heat of the day being at its worst, it was a lot. Way more than me. He walked in an awkward, peculiar way too, taking careful, but stuttering half-skip steps that caused his back to be slumped forward one second, then drawn back the next. His eyes were closed to narrow slits, and his nose was long, thin, and pointed. He appeared to be trying to whistle but couldn't quite hit the note. His lips just gushed air in and out. Despite his bizarre gait, he moved at a brisk pace towards us. Joe watched as the Stranger got to the sidewalk on the other side of the street and passed in front of his yard.

Joe never took his eyes off of him, but he waved Willie up. "Come here, son."

Willie left the sandbox once more and dashed to the porch, ever eager to please his granddaddy.

"That fella got you a little spooked, don't he?" I asked, even though he surely had me spooked.

"He's got no business 'round here, walking around like that."

"Maybe he's drunk. He probably crossed the tracks to go to the liquor store." I said that knowing full-well he didn't.

"Then he's taking the long way. 'Sides, he didn't cross no tracks. He just appeared there under that ol' tree. One second, he wasn't there. Next second, he was, sure as the world."

Well now, that part I doubted just a bit. "Maybe he hopped off the train last night and slept up in the tree like a Chimpanese monkey."

"Oh, come on, man. He didn't do that." Joe pulled Willie up onto his lap. "I don't like him being here." The next thing he said, he nearly spit. I'll never forget it. "He got a jagged nose."

"It's a little out of joint, I reckon," I said. I had to squint to see the details of his face. His nose was crooked, sure. But jagged? Seemed an extreme description.

"Out of joint nothing. It's a jagged thing." There was no simple hint of vitriol in his tone. It was pure hatred on full display.

"He's just a wandering ol' fool." I said it to calm Joe, but I didn't let my eyes leave him either. The better look I got of him though, the less I could see him as a threat. In fact, I started to wonder if I even had that dream the night before. Maybe I had a quick imagining of it when I first saw the guy, like a déjà vu or something where the subconscious mind works a little faster than the conscious one. I was at an age where my thoughts were never a certain thing anyway. My memories weren't either. Maybe I was just buying into Joe's fear of the pitiful dude in our neighborhood and conjured a memory of a dream to make it make sense. "Leave him be, Joe, and he'll find his way back to somewhere else."

"He does one wrong thing and I'm calling the law, ya hear?"

I stood up then. The Stranger scrambled on down the sidewalk and was in front of Felicia's when I got to the rail of Joe's porch.

"C'mon, forget that guy. Let's go fire up the smoker. We need to start those ribs," I advised as I went down the steps and out into the yard.

Joe remained on the porch, uneasy. He kept watching the Stranger. Willie, happy that one of his old caretakers was up and appearing to be doing something, hopped out of Joe's lap and hurried down next to me. I felt his little grip on the pinky finger of my right hand. Joe stood up and leaned on his porch's railing, his eyes still locked on the Stranger jigging and side-stepping down the way.

He went beyond Felicia's and past my house. He was moving along, and he didn't do a thing to any of the three houses that mattered to us. He wasn't near the problem we were making him out to be after all. Crisis averted. Ribs to smoke. Dream irrelevant and forgotten. *Let's go.*

I looked up at Joe. He was still on the porch at the top of the steps. His face was a contortion that revealed his maligned spirit. Willie tugged my finger, ready to find an adventure elsewhere. I let him lead me around the side of Joe's house toward the back-yard. We left his granddaddy there, staring after the Stranger.

I knew Joe Moore for as long as I could remember. I wish I'd introduced him on any other day than when that skinny, white man came walking down Doreen Street. I wish I could have better shown him to be the way I always knew him. There are stories I could tell that could illuminate a little better to who he really was. At the best of times, he was a modern prophet, and I was his eager apostle.

Joe and I made a habit of sitting in the rockers on his porch, late into the evenings. We would smoke cigars and sip from tumblers. A bottle of Old Red's Bourbon and an ashtray would be on the small table between us. We'd get pleasantly drunk and we'd just talk. This became a once or twice a week occurrence for many years.

Sometimes we'd talk about baseball or fishing. Other times we'd tackle the big subjects. Like this one time in particular.

"Drinking whiskey and talking 'bout God. You think we should be mixing the two?" I'd said that night.

"If it broadens our imagination, then why not? Sobriety leads to dull, dim-witted thinking. How do you think the Greeks came up with all those mythologies?" Joe was smiling when he spoke. Missing tooth front and center, happy to be seen.

"The Greeks?" I chuckled at that.

"You ever tried seeing those zodiacs in the stars at night? Have a glass or two. All those creatures and hunters and dippers will pop out sure as the world."

"Man, you crazy!" I didn't mean it, of course. Just more joking around.

That night, Joe went from playing to giving me something true. Something I would never forget. "All I'm saying is God made us different. He gave us the ability to ask questions and seek answers. And what do we do? We set up big, barbed wire fences in our brains. The only limits we have are the ones we make for ourselves." He was ramping up.

"Come on now! Preach it, baby! Preach it!" I'd heard myself say with a couple of stomps of my feet. Joe was at his best when he was talking passionately about something.

"My daughter, I want her to think on her own and use whatever I've taught her to make her own decisions. It was up to me to raise her right, then turn her a-loose. I don't want her to be a mindless robot who does whatever I say or follows whatever path I set out for her. I want her to see things I haven't seen and do things I haven't done and live places I never lived! I want her to find her own way and make her own life! I imagine God would want the same for all of us!"

Another night, we got to talking about all the social discord in the world. He claimed that there was an easy fix. "We just got to do one thing for one another. When we see someone, we owe them a friendly nod or smile. Better yet, we owe them both. That's it. We don't have to walk anywhere in anyone's shoes or instantly understand every tragedy they've ever suffered. That expectation is too much and unsustainable. Just a genuinely friendly nod or a smile is all that's needed. We do that, then we'll hopefully get one in return. That opens the door for deeper conversation and learning about each other and understanding the other person's experiences. Real relationships can grow from there. Or maybe they don't and that's fine, too. We can't demand people respect each other's story before they know it. We just have to be friendly and cordial and then we can build from there."

That was the Joe Moore I knew. Someway, somehow, everything he'd say always made sense to me. Even without the Ol' Red's.

Chapter 4

Joe was standing against the rail, still looking down the road. Willie was by me, holding my hand and tugging me on toward the backyard. I couldn't help but stand firm. I was looking at Joe because doubt had crept in on me. I doubted that I ever had that dream. In fact, I'd convinced myself it was a conjured-up figment. If there was no premonition, then I could only judge that Stranger by what I'd seen of him now that I'd had a chance to see him in the daylight.

He was pitiful and sad and quite possibly drug-addled and not a thing in the world to be worried about. Joe hadn't reached that conclusion yet, and that contradicted what he claimed he believed about a friendly nod and smile. His preoccupation with the Stranger, which was quickly becoming an obsession in my eyes, was the reason for my concern.

"Will you forget ol' Hobo-Joe already?" I said, finally letting Willie move me.

"Man, how come 'cuz he's a hobo he gotta be named 'Joe'?" he said, still not breaking his gaze away from the Stranger.

"You right. You right. He probably got him a good hobo name. Something like Charley Chuckup. Or Saltfish Swanson."

That made Joe shake his head, and finally pulled him from the attention vortex that the Stranger had become. Joe stepped down from the porch and walked past me and Willie toward the backyard. Willie tugged me on as if we had to beat Joe back there.

"Percy Polecat," I said, keeping with my hobo-themed train of thought. "Henry Honey-truck. Chester Chisholm Cheesewheel the Third!"

A minute or two later, Joe was chopping thin hickory-log pieces into smaller chunks with a hatchet and tossing them into a wood pile by his smoker. He was trying his best to ignore me, but I was really rolling by then.

"Itchy Ben. Jeffy Dumpster-jump. Fleabee Jeeves. Timmy Gristle."

Later, Joe stoked a fire in the smoker with the hickory chunks and I was standing by holding Willie on my hip so he could look down at what his grandaddy was doing. I still hadn't lost my head of steam.

"Bean Can Lenny or Freddy Fatback or Leon Scrap-happy!" The names were coming to me from nowhere and I was finding every one of them quite hilarious. Michael Jordan and Moham-mad Ali lived their lives in a place known as 'The Zone' where hard things came easy and they appeared to be running a wind-assisted race when everyone else was in knee-deep water. In that stretch of moments, I was getting a glimpse of what that was like.

Joe just kept shaking his head.

Somehow, we ended up back on the porch, though I was so focused that I didn't know when or how. Joe was by the rail, looking for the Stranger again. Willie was on the floor at Joe's feet with a toy truck. I was in the chair behind them both.

"Stewkettle Earl. Rattlewagon Sinclair. Sump-pump Sammy the Ramshackle Man."

Joe lifted a pair of binoculars and aimed them down the street.

"Hey, when'd you get the binocs?" I asked him, thoroughly surprised to see their sudden appearance.

"Somewhere between Otis Onion-bags and Jimmy John Scurvy Scab," Joe said. I don't know if I had named those off or if they were Joe's contributions, but they seemed like a good place to end all things hobo and exit the mystical 'Zone'.

I looked down at Willie. He sure could make me happy. I was already feeling good about things and getting on with a pretty good day after a rough start. His little transcendent smile up at me only made everything a thousand times better.

"God Almighty, that's a handsome boy right there."

Chapter 5

Some parts of that day, I wasn't there for, so I've had to reconstruct what happened through conversation with those who were present. Hopefully, I haven't filled in too many of the details with my own imaginings.

While I was making up hobo names and Joe was prepping the smoker, Felicia and Yvette sat on one side of a large table in a hospital conference room. Maybe it was a doctor's office, but that doesn't really matter. What's important was that Doctor Dawkins, a tall black man in his 30s, sat next to Felicia. Dr. Anderson, a congenial white fellow about mine and Joe's age, sat on the other side. A third doctor that was supposed to be there didn't show. She had to perform an emergency surgery or something.

There was a thick medical file open on the table in front of Felicia. It was Willie's and it held fifty or so pages of the saddest story ever told.

"Felicia," Dr. Dawkins said. "Doctor Anderson is the best pediatric neurosurgeon in the state. He's reviewed the scans. The other day, you and I talked about best and worst-case scenarios." Felicia reached onto the table and grasped his hand. He didn't need to continue, but he did. "I'm afraid..."

Felicia gripped his hand tightly. She was near tears, but her tone said she was mad as blazes. "Oh no! No, you don't! Just a few days ago, you said you were relieved it was so small! Don't you be going back on that! Don't you be saying 'I'm afraid!'"

"I was relieved. Initially." Dr. Dawkins tried keeping it professional. He was calm and empathetic. "Nine times out of ten, tumors are more easily treated if caught early. But sometimes--"

"Sometimes what?" Felicia was too much like her Daddy. Usually at the wrong times. She pointed at Dr. Anderson with the hand that wasn't clenching Dr. Dawkins. "You said he would operate!"

Dr. Anderson swooped in to save Dr. Dawkins from Felicia's ire. "Ma'am, this tumor is growing extremely fast. It's what we call a 'grade four glioblastoma'. Now, it worries me for several reasons. Obviously, the speed with which it's growing is problematic. But, just as importantly, the location is a major concern. Most worrisome though, is the shape. It's a long, thin tumor, like a finger."

"Which means what?" Felicia barked.

"It means it's very difficult to perform the procedure I was hoping to perform. More likely than not, we won't be able to reach it without doing irreparable damage."

"Then, isn't there some kind of medicine you can give him to shrink it. Radiation or something?"

Dr. Dawkins answered that one. "Radiation won't slow a tumor growing this fast."

Felicia, bless her soul, wanted to find where to lay the blame and she wanted confirmation to her suspicion that the finger in Willie's brain was pointing at her. "How did this happen to my baby? What did I do wrong?"

"Nothing caused it. It's just there." Dr. Anderson was a little too matter-of-fact. Dr. Dawkins knew what Felicia needed so he hugged her close to him, put his head against hers, and shook it so that hers shook, too.

"You didn't do this. Nobody did. It's nobody's fault. Least of all, yours."

Felicia let go of all the tears she was holding back then. Felicia accepted her sorrow, but Yvette, seeing her own baby in anguish, reached the anger phase. "There has to be another center that can look at him. We'll take him to another state and to a better hospital! We'll take him out of the country if we need to! There's got to be a doctor somewhere who will do the surgery he needs!"

"The stress of traveling and undergoing another battery of tests will do more harm to him than good," Dr. Anderson answered. If he was insulted, he didn't show it. "It's inoperable, Missus Moore. He'll die if I try to operate. No reputable doctor will touch him."

Dr. Dawkins reached around Felicia as she sobbed into his shoulder. He grabbed Yvette and pulled her to Felicia so they were in a three-person wide embrace.

Dr. Anderson saw the situation for what it was, felt like he was intruding, and quietly got up. "I'm so sorry. Truly, I am. Please believe me when I say we have looked at this from every possible angle. If there was anything we could do, we would do it." With that, he left.

Felicia bawled. "I don't know what to do. Tell me what to do for my baby boy."

"Keep him calm and love him with all of your might," Dr. Dawkins said.

Yvette wasn't ready to concede defeat. She jerked away from the group hug. "And wait for him to die?" She shook her head. "That's your advice?"

"Willie needs to see you laughing," he said over Felicia's head to Yvette. He had tears building in his eyes by then, too. "At his age, he doesn't know his body is failing him."

"How much time does he have?" Yvette stood and paced around the table.

"There's no way to tell. The fact that he's stopped talking in the last few days means the tumor is putting more pressure on his brain. As it gets worse, he'll lose his motor skills and his ability to walk."

"Stop talking doctor to me! Your friend is gone!" Like I said, Yvette could be quite a spitfire when she wanted to be. "How much time?"

"A week or two. A month at the most." With that being said, the tears welling in Dr. Dawkins's eyes let loose and rolled down his cheeks.

And so, finally, did Yvette's.

Chapter 6

On the porch, Joe was still at the rail, looking down the road through the binoculars. Willie was back in the sandbox, and I was rocking in the chair, thinking that it had to be getting about time for Ol' Red.

"Good Lord, Joe, will you leave it alone? I'm telling you, he's gone."

"Oh no, he ain't," Joe argued. "He just did an about face down yonder and is coming back this way."

I stood up and went to his side. "Let me see them things." I looked through the binoculars.

"Right there. Down by Ida's house," Joe said.

"He stopped right in front of it."

"She ain't home, I don't believe." Joe snatched them from me and took another look.

"Take 'em then," I said in protest. "I don't care no way." I sat back down like I really didn't care, but there probably was a little bit of a pout element to it. I'll at least admit that much. "You crazy for spying on an 'ol vagrant anyway. Being nosy is all. You an old lady!"

Joe wasn't listening to me. "He just walked right through Ida's gate and touched the corner of her house! Why'd he go and do that?"

"I don't know, Joe. I can't see him, 'member? You stole the binocs from me. Is he still walking funny?"

"He sure is."

"I'm telling ya, he's a drunk. Or on meth or crack. Maybe he crushed up Oxy and snorted it. They do that nowadays, you know?"

"He's leaving. Just touched the side of her house and walked away. Didn't even knock." Joe walked over and handed the binoculars to me then. "Tell me if you see Ida drive by. I'm gonna go find my phone and leave her a message just in case something comes up missing."

I took the binoculars and looked. "There ain't nothing to say really. He just went to her house. Salespeople do that all the time. Girl Scouts. Little League players looking for donations. Jehovah's Witness."

"Where's his clipboard? Where's his cookies or catcher's mitt or Bible? For cryin' out loud, he don't look like any of those," Joe sniped.

"He's walking this way again," I said. "He's over to the Haynes's place. They ain't home neither, I don't think. He's touching their front door."

"That's it. I'm calling the police." Joe started back inside to retrieve his phone.

"Naw, relax. He ain't trying to break in. He's just..." I wasn't quite sure what to say next because the Stranger pressed his hand flat against the door just below the little window. "He's just laying hands on it."

Joe snatched the binoculars from me again at that point. "Gimme those!" He peered through them. "He sure enough is! Walking back across the street, skipping and zigzagging along, like he's dancing or something."

I squinted down the road to try and keep up with the play-by-play, but I could barely see anything. I just sat back down and patted my face with my handkerchief.

"Now he's heading over to your nephew's."

"Manny?" I asked. Joe also insisted on calling him my nephew even though he really wasn't. "He ain't my nephew. That boy is Trina's kin. Ain't nothing but rotten either. Got all the sorry blood in her family. He still out there washing his car?" I jumped up again to try and see.

"Yep, and you know he's got that temper. Mister Jagged Man gonna be the sorry one if he walks up on Manny."

Sure enough, the Stranger did. Manny was hosing off his car in his driveway when the Stranger ambled within ten feet of him. The Stranger didn't seem to notice Manny at all. Manny noticed him, though. At first, he watched the Stranger with consternation that he would have the audacity to approach his yard. Then, Manny got flat out mad when the Stranger kept walking until he was right up on the house. He placed his hand on the front wall, closed his eyes, and became still for several seconds. By then, Manny had barked at him, asking him what he thought he was doing. When the Stranger didn't respond in any way, Manny flung down the hose and ran up on him. He was just inches away from the Stranger when he barked again, loud enough for me and Joe to hear him way down the road.

"Hey, crackhead!"

The Stranger turned his head slowly and awkwardly without turning his body. He looked like an owl.

"Yeah, I'm talking to you!" we heard Manny say. "What're you doing touching on my house?"

Joe was still watching through the binoculars. He couldn't help but grin. "What'd I tell ya? Betcha Manny busts him good."

I couldn't see too well, and Manny wasn't talking loud anymore, so I depended on Joe's commentary to keep me up to date. He didn't say anything for a good while, though.

"Well," I said, expecting something.

"I'll be," is all Joe said, real low, like he was talking to himself and not me.

"What's he doing?" Even though I asked loud enough that I knew he heard me, Joe still didn't say a word. "C'mon, Joe, what's he doing?"

Finally, in disbelief, Joe said, "That creep just shook Manny's hand."

"He did what?" Now that was impossible to understand, knowing Manny the way I did.

"Yes, sir. Manny smiled and said something back real slow. They are still shaking hands, too. Way too long, if you ask me. Manny looks hypnotized or something."

"Manny must be on those pills again. Eleven thirty on a Friday morning and he's already strung out. Maybe he's Manny's dealer."

"Or vicey versy," Joe mumbled.

All I could do was shake my head and mop off my brow again. "Good Lord, it's hot." It was. It really, really was. I was losing interest again since nothing juicy happened between Manny and the Stranger. I sat back down and looked out at Willie. "Keeps himself entertained really good, don't he?" That boy could surely bring a grin to my face.

Either Joe didn't hear or he didn't care, one. He kept peering at the Stranger through the binoculars. "Looks like he's heading over to Jamal and Evelyn's place." A moment passed. Joe chuckled. "Now Jamal's yelling at him. He's shooing him off like a coon in the trash."

About then, the Stranger got face to face with Jamal Sheldon, who was a lean, lanky fellow like me, but nearly half my age. Jamal stood like a gatekeeper on the top step of his porch.

"Go on, you! Go and get on down the road!" Jamal sounded tough, but he was a sweet dude who wouldn't hurt a fly. I knew if Manny hadn't popped that Stranger, then Jamal wouldn't either. Joe was hopeful, though. He cheered Jamal on, like he was rooting for a boxer in the ring. I didn't even bother to try and watch. Instead, I just kept looking down at Willie while he played.

That's when Jamal's wife, Evelyn, came out the front door to most likely see what Jamal had been yelling about. She and Jamal became still as the Stranger ascended the steps and reached out to touch them both on the shoulder. As if in a trance, they joined hands, turned and went inside as the Stranger touched a column on the front porch on his way down the steps. And that was that. Off he went, back to the road, toward Joe's house and the old oak.

Joe was trembling when he saw all of that. So much so, he could barely hold the binoculars to his eyes anymore. He lowered them to the railing, so I took them from him and had a look, if for no other reason than to keep his shaking hands from dropping them in the grass below.

Looking through the spyglasses, I saw little Daizy Mae run up to the Stranger, dragging her sun-bleached leash behind her. She sat down in front of him. He stopped and looked down at her for the longest moment, as if time had paused, before he finally stooped down to stroke her head.

Beside me, I felt Joe wilt a bit and he leaned heavily on the railing, almost like his knees had buckled and he had to catch himself. To see Joe acting so scared of that Stranger just didn't seem right. Quite frankly, it made me question why I wasn't more afraid myself. In all the years I'd known him, Joe wasn't ever scared of anything. Especially another man.

But then again, that day was turning out to be unlike one I'd ever lived. I'm sure Joe would have said the same.

Chapter 7

When I say Joe wasn't scared of other men, I mean it. He wasn't even frightened by his father-in-law. Which, knowing that old curmudgeon the way I did, is saying a lot.

Joe was twenty when he asked for Yvette's hand in marriage. He rang her Daddy before he asked her though, and met him at our local drugstore. I worked there in the afternoons. My title was Soda Fountain Attendant, but some people, namely Joe, insisted on calling me a Soda Jerk. He always emphasized the second part and routinely left out the first part all together.

Joe arranged to meet there because he figured I'd have his back if things went sideways, which was always a real possibility with Yvette's old man. Joe arrived first. He was well dressed (suit, tie, the whole nine), as if he had just come from church. He waited by the door for Yvette's father.

At fifty years of age or so, her father was a big, husky, stern man who could strike fear in the most hardcore of men. He was black, of course, but lighter in skin tone than Joe. He didn't so much as enter the store as conquer it. He blasted through the doors, totally ignored Joe, and went straight to the dining area. Joe gave me a shrug as he fell in behind him.

Yvette's father sat at the table and Joe smiled when he took the seat across from him, showing off his full set of pearly whites. He only got a scowl in reply. I watched intently from my station behind the counter. They skipped the ice cream and Yvette's dad ordered two coffees from the waitress before she even got to their table.

"So, you wanna marry my daughter?" The old codger didn't have much thought for small talk. He just cut right to it.

"Yes, sir, I do," Joe said. "But only with your permission and blessing."

"Joe, I've known you a good while now, and I gotta admit, I like you." Joe smiled at that. He was off to a good start. "You seem smart enough and you treat my daughter rightly. But let me tell you why I can't allow this union to happen and I'm going to be blunt."

When an already blunt man says he's going to be blunt, then a nuclear missile is incoming. Joe knew it. He swallowed hard and braced himself. And Yvette's father didn't disappoint.

"You're just too black, son. Plain and simple, too black. You're as black as they come and, in this day and age, the color of a man's skin says it all. Therefore, I'll have my say on the matter and my say is that's the end of it."

Joe was quick to protest. "But Mister--"

"Now, hear me out, son," Yvette's father interrupted. "I know it ain't your fault. Both of your parents might be just as black as you as far as I can tell. And I know it's a terrible thing for me to say, but you gotta start seeing things for what they are. What do you think white America sees when they look at you?" He paused long enough to allow that ruthless little tick of a query to dig under Joe's skin and burrow all the way into his bloodstream. Then, as if he hadn't been condescending enough, he said, "Now I know better and you know you better, but they don't, and their opinions are the ones that make us or break us. I can't knowingly subject Yvette to that kind of life, and I certainly can't let that sort of prejudice be passed on to my grandchildren."

I had stepped in for the waitress by then and took their two cups of coffee to their table, along with some sugar and cream.

As I set the dishes down, Yvette's father didn't look up. He just said, "Thank you, darlin'."

When he saw that it was me and not the waitress he had ordered from, he looked aghast. Not an embarrassed aghast. No, it was an angry aghast. I felt his glare freeze my soul. Had I been older, I might have given him a sarcastic reply of some sort to get him off his game and help Joe gain some ground, but that wasn't what I did. I just scuttled off without saying a word, thankful to get out of there without a throttling.

While the surly fellow stared me into submissive retreat, Joe grabbed both cups of coffee. When Yvette's dad saw, he intensified his scorching glare at Joe.

"What're you doing? I gotta certain way I like my coffee, son. Best push it back across the table now." I felt like running over and giving him back the cup myself.

"With all due respect, sir. It's your turn to hear me out," Joe smiled as his eyes stayed locked on his future father-in-law's. The gruff old thing looked back at Joe with a steely gaze that said more than his mouth ever could. It said that he was curious about how Joe could keep such a level head after being told he was too black for a black man's daughter. It also said he wouldn't take much in the way of reciprocal disrespect.

"Try this," Joe said, finally pushing one of the cups to Yvette's father. "Just like it is."

The man glowered, which was becoming pretty clear was his default expression, but he decided to play along.

"We'll call this cup 'Joe-style'," Joe added.

Yvette's father took a reluctant sip, then dropped the cup back to the table. Coffee sloshed out, but he didn't care. It's almost like he did it on purpose in a symbolic gesture.

"It's too bold. Too acidic. Too black." He seethed the words, enjoying the hurt he hoped they inflicted. "Wouldn't waste my dog's time on this swill."

"Yes, it is rough stuff to be sure." Joe was still smiling, seemingly ignoring the parallel that was being drawn. Instead of taking offense at the backhanded insult though, Joe just heaped four tablespoons of sugar into the cream decanter, then filled it to the brim with half of the coffee from the second cup.

"What on God's green earth are you doing?" Yvette's father barked.

It was loud enough to draw everyone's attention to the table, including the waitress. She got pretty incensed that Joe had ruined a cup of cream, but I held her back by her arm when she made a break toward them. I shook my head as a plea to allow the little drama at table four to play on out. Thankfully, she did.

Joe stirred the cream and coffee and sugar until it blended into a nice, light tan color. Still smiling, he pushed it across the table.

"This is guaranteed to make your lips dance," Joe beamed.

The father took the decanter from him. "I guess this is 'Yvette-style', huh?" In fact, the creamy tan color nearly matched her skin tone perfectly. He grasped it by the handle and, in a manner that I found quite funny since he was still trying to be tough, sipped from the little spout. He might as well have raised his pinky. "It's sweet. Rich. Smooth." The man wasn't about to talk bad about his daughter.

"And full bodied. Don't forget the wonderful full body." Joe slipped that in as a jab, I'm sure. Yvette's dad warned him off from pursuing that further with a severe grimace. Joe rolled on. "But could you drink that whole cup? You gotta admit, that cup of coffee has a flair for drama. Sweet, yes, but boy oh boy can it jump fast into the high altitude of attitude. It can cut to the quick too, and take no prisoners when it gets upset or angry, can't it?"

Yvette's dad softened his stare at Joe. Joe was speaking the truth, and the old man knew it. He raised a buzzsaw of a daugh-

ter. The fact that he didn't argue Joe's point told me, and everyone listening, that she had sharpened her claws on him while
she was growing up. She tested her wit against his and had of-
tentimes come out on top.

Joe took the decanter from in front of the man and held it by
the remaining coffee in the second cup.

"Now you see, ol' 'Joe-style' is helpless all alone. Just gonna
sit there and turn stale 'til somebody finally throws him out.
And 'Yvette-style, well, she is perfect. Surely, perfect. But even
she could use something to calm her boldness and curb her
sweetness. Now, ol' Joe can do that. He can balance her. And
she, well…" Joe carefully poured half of the decanter's contents
into the cup, blending it into a deep, caramel brown. "She's the
only thing that can make ol' Joe any good at all. He makes her a
bit better. She makes him worlds better."

He mixed the cup with the spoon and let the tinkle of it echo
through the quiet diner for a couple of seconds. Then, he slid it
across the table to Yvette's father, who showed his hand when
he was a little too eager to sip it. He had bought into the illusion
Joe had created and was eager to reach the conclusion. Joe had
won him over by then, plain and simple. We all knew it.

"Nicely balanced. Not too sweet. Not too bold. Nice caramel
color, too," he said. He put the cup down. When he looked at
Joe again, all the pretense and intimidation tactics were gone.
What was left was a man asking another man to be honest, because a lie would hurt the most precious thing in his world.
"You're a clever boy, Joe, but so is every card shark and hustler
and snake oil salesman I ever met. How do I know you're right
for my daughter?"

Joe didn't hesitate. "Because I love her and I'll never let her
down. She'll get my best, all the time. She'll be the queen of my
kingdom and the goddess of my temple. I will be to her what
you are to her momma. And that is my vow to you, sir."

Yvette's father leaned back in his seat and folded his arms. He was back to acting like he was still thinking it over.

"And I promise to give you a carload of beautiful caramel-colored grandchildren." Joe added that because he always tried to close with a joke. He was good at that.

Yvette's father huffed, then leaned forward again. "So, I'm supposed to overlook everything I already said about your color and what that means?"

Joe shrugged off the comment like he knew it was coming. "You know, the color black ain't caused by the absence of light, but the absorption of it."

"What's that supposed to mean?"

"Well, sir, it means I'm full of light."

Finally, the hard facade on Yvette's father cracked and a smile broke through. "Oh, you're full of something," he chortled. Seeing him laugh was like seeing an alligator climb a Weeping Willow.

Yvette's father looked at Joe a moment more, then he stretched his wide, beefy hand across the table. They shook and the marriage proposal proceeded, and Joe was everything he said he would be as a husband and that was the end of that.

Chapter 8

I led Willie by the hand to the sandbox. Willie got in and sat down and patted the sand next to him with a big grin. I hated to see that. The little fellow was so cute. I couldn't resist sitting in the sand next to him, but that's the last thing in the world my old body wanted to do. It took me a bit to wrangle my pants up enough so I could squat. It took a while longer to get down to a full seated position by him. My hips and knees popped so loud I guess I'm lucky nobody called the cops and reported a drive-by shooting.

Willie was so happy that I eased down next to him that he filled his plastic bucket with sand and poured it in my lap. I laughed. Who wouldn't with that impossibly adorable child smiling up at them? As I wiped the sand from my legs, he went about revving his toy truck through the mini sand dunes he had conjured with his shovel.

On the porch, Joe was still watching the Stranger. I was watching him when he looked down at me.

"You're gonna get sand in your dungarees," he said in a dull, listless way.

"I done did, my friend," I said. "I'm just a cat carrying a big ol' litter box around with me in my drawers. It's real convenient."

That didn't elicit much of a response from Joe. He just looked back down the road. I scooped sand with my hands and helped Willie fill his bucket again. When we got it done, back in my lap it went. Willie giggled hard. Joe ambled down the steps and stood over us, near the box.

"He ain't supposed to laugh so hard." Joe leaned in and grabbed Willie under the arms and lifted him out of the box. I felt a little like he was punishing me for entertaining the boy.

"Well, Willie says you're being a nervous ol' bitty! He told me so. That's what had him laughing."

Willie grinned at that. I stood up amidst another barrage of cracks and pops and a scream of protest from my back. I rubbed Willie's head until he laughed again and Joe turned him away from me.

"You gotta stop making him laugh, bubba. It increases the pressure in his brain."

"The pressure in your brain is high on account of your head being so far up your hooty pooty."

Joe wasn't in the joking mood.

"Shoot, man," I said. "I remember when you weren't bothered by any white dude who crossed those tracks. Why's that ol' tweaker got you so worked up?"

"There were days when I was bolder, weren't there?"

"Me, too, I guess. Heck, back in the day, we was Achilles and Hector."

"They were enemies. We weren't."

That's when I knew for sure Joe wasn't himself. The Hector and Achilles thing was a long-running joke between us. Years before, Joe had read The Iliad and told me I should read it too, telling me it was the greatest story ever written. I struggled all the way through it and felt like I was in an extended torture scene in one of Schwarzenegger's movies (all of which I liked way better than that book). We were smoking cigars one night when I told him I had finished it. He forgot all about it because it had taken me six months to get through. Boy, did he laugh.

"You actually read that?" he whooped.

I confirmed that I did indeed.

"Man, that book was rough. Had to have been six million men in that war. Heck, ten thousand a day died at the hands of one hero or another for ten years! And Achilles brooded like a prissy prima donna and Hector cowered like a beaten raccoon before he even took to the final battle!"

I stomped my foot in laughter. "He was shaking like a dog passing a peach seed!"

With that, he confessed he hated it as much as I did. "They didn't even talk about the wooden horse!"

"Why'd you tell me to read it then? 'Cuz misery loves company?"

"Nah. 'Cuz it's important. We thought we knew that story all our lives. Turns out, we really didn't. Not until we read it for ourselves. They told us it was great. We believed them. Maybe it is to some folks, but I didn't care for it and neither did you. But we learned from it for sure. We learned that heroes aren't always brave or fearless, so we shouldn't expect that of ourselves. We learned that the most pivotal part of a story, the thing that's most remembered and most often quoted, might only be a single, passing sentence or not even be in there at all, like the horse. That's why we got to do things ourselves. Taste escargot and caviar and that goose liver stuff. We got to see the countries and monuments that flood our history books and hear the languages that preceded our own spoken in their home countries by the people that live there. We got to read the Bible so the pastor can't tell us what we should think about God when God gave us the power to make up our minds ourselves. We're always a little more enlightened when we're willing to go after the things we've never seen or confront the things that scare us. To get better, sometimes we have to dive into the belly of the beast, you know what I mean?"

"Yeah, I do. And that book was a beast for sure."

"Wait until you read The Odyssey. Now that's a book!"

"Uh huh. The onliest Homer I ever need again is Simpson! Talk about a genius!"

We laughed some more. Our joke always went that, when we were talking about our mightier days, I'd say we were like Achilles and Hector. And Joe would agree and say we were the best of brothers, like Cain and Abel.

It was stupid, but it was our joke and we usually did it around people that barely knew us. Anyone within earshot would just roll their eyes at us if they heard it. Maybe they thought we were simple-minded or uneducated thanks to our shabby clothes and cheap cigars. Maybe they wouldn't guess we had seen the things we had seen and done the things we had done and that was because they didn't take the time to get to know us. And that was the point, after all.

"You never know nothing until you learn it yourself."

Joe always said that. It was an important part of his philosophy for two reasons. One, as I already explained, it's required for growth and expansion of self. A smart man will learn things on his own. The other half of that double-edged sword, so to speak, was that a man can learn, but mankind can't. Humans are smart, but humanity is dumb, because humanity insists on doing things itself and learning (or not) the same thing over and over.

Joe used to say that was the reason the Bible and stories like The Iliad still appealed to people. The stories were known to humans and were practically part of their DNA by current times, but humanity still carried on as if they were brand new. Civilization evolves. We develop new tools for living. New gadgets. New ways to make our lives easier and, hopefully, more enriched. But the tales of people from 6000 years ago still resonate because civilizations evolve, but its citizens don't.

At its core, the Bible is about human nature. Greed, lust, power, anger, jealousy, all those innate human traits. We commit the sins of our fathers like they committed those of theirs. We know the stories. Adultery leads to pain and suffering for all parties. Every single time. But people still do it every day, thinking they know the pitfalls and how to avoid them. Jealousy creates havoc in relationships, but somewhere, right now, someone is punching a wall over something they think was done against them behind their back. Greed is a killer. Vengeance is a dead-end street. On and on it goes. Hatred devolves everything into chaos.

Love is the answer. We know this, but every generation calls it something new and acts like they came up with a brilliant new concept and puts it in songs or movies or books and people devour it and swear they'll apply it and practice it and the world will change. We've known from the beginning that love is the answer to all that plagues us. And yet we insist on forgetting it and burying it until the next Renaissance of thought on the subject.

So, the Bible and Homer and Shakespeare and all things old remain relevant. And we stay where we are, but with fancy new TVs and phones and embedded satellite dishes in our Medulla Oblongatas (or whatever is next).

"You never know nothing until you learn it yourself."

That's the truth. The good of it and the bad.

Chapter 9

Achilles and Hector. That's how old men think of their younger selves. They sit around and talk about when they were bolder. Smarter. Braver. Better. They think of their finest hours, long past, and embellish them into grandiose tales of amazing triumph.

Joe had stories worth repeating. The thing is, he never repeated them. Other people did. That's the difference between Joe and fraudsters. A real hero never talks about his victories. Other people do. A fake hero is typically the only one to talk about his achievements and other people may have heard the lore, but don't know anyone else who was actually there to see it.

Joe had a few finest hours and I was there to see them.

One came when a mob of twenty white men marched up Doreen Street. They were armed with metal pipes, bats, broomsticks, and other yard tools-turned weapons. They carried flashlights and a few, I kid you not, put forth the effort to make torches and paraded with them. The irony was that it was dark when they came and had been for hours and they probably used flashlights to find the stuff in their sheds to make the torches. But, hey, some people take their role-playing to the extreme.

Same thing goes for the robes. They weren't KKK robes. They were just white sheets with eye holes cut in them and more than a few of those men felt like they had to wear them.

I'd like to say their arrival took us by surprise, but we expected them. Things were getting better in our town in the early-seventies and those white men were our lifelong neigh-bors, but we still expected them.

It was in the spring of 1972. One of the boys from a street near Doreen had beaten and raped a girl earlier that afternoon. A white girl. The boy was already in jail, but that didn't stop the hate from coming over from that side of town like a tsunami.

I was on my poor excuse for a porch when a teenager from further down Doreen Street crossed the railroad tracks a few minutes ahead of the mob. He was yelling as loud as he could for all to hear.

"They're coming! They're coming!"

I was in my twenties and was a tall, strapping dude back then. I had been in more than a few scrapes and I wasn't one to back down from a fight. My reaction was predictable. I grabbed an ax and shouldered it.

Since Joe's house was the first on the block, my immediate concern was for him and Yvette, so I sprinted toward his place as the teenager went the other way down the road, our own Paul Revere, telling us the invasion was imminent.

His house was dark, so I didn't see him on his porch until he spoke. "Evenin', bubba. Planning on chopping down a tree at this late hour?" he asked.

I had adrenaline pumping through me, so his quiet question was returned with a yelled answer. "The Klan's 'bout to cross the tracks! Best get Yvette outta here! Your house is the first they're gonna see, and if they've a mind to tear something up, it'll be your place straight away!"

Joe walked down from his porch, and got where he could see down the road to the other side of the tracks. Their angry shouts and the light from their flashlights and the few torches (somehow that still cracks me up) preceded them.

"The Klan, huh?" Joe asked. He was in his twenties, too, and much shorter, of course, than me.

I'd never known him to get in a scrap, but he never backed down from one. Joe had a philosophy on fighting, just as he did on most other things. He said he was a wolverine in a world of grizzlies. A grizzly can demolish and eat just about anything it wants because it's so big and so well equipped by nature to enforce its will on everything around it. Joe was small compared to most guys, just as a wolverine is miniscule next to a grizzly. A grizzly, though, will go out of its way to avoid a wolverine. The reason is simple. A wolverine is too fierce. Sure, a grizzly will eventually kill it and eat it, but it's going to get scratched and bitten by the wolverine until the bitter end. Some of those scratches and bites will be deep and they might get infected. The grizzly might even lose an eye in the ordeal. The bear knows the end result isn't worth it. The wolverine is too small to be much of a meal, so why suffer through a bunch of wounds to get an insubstantial win? Grizzlies see a wolverine and turn the other way.

That's how Joe carried himself around bigger, stronger men. They knew they could take him in the long run, but they also knew they'd walk away with damage that they didn't need. Especially when the final result would be other guys sarcastically saying, "Wow, you beat a smaller man. Good for you, tough guy, but look at your face. How many of your fingers are bent the wrong way? How long before that bite gets infected? What do you make of that maple syrup stuff oozing from your eye?"

"Grab a shovel or a bat!" I hollered even though he was right beside me. My adrenaline was pumping hard.

By then, the street was filled with other men from surrounding homes. Joe paid me no mind. I had warned him, as was my duty as his friend, but I realized that was all I owed him. What he did to protect himself and his young bride was up to him. I turned and joined the other men.

"Here we go, boys! Here we go!" I remember yelling the words, like the fight was something that I wanted and was eager to dive into. It makes me twitch with embarrassment when I think back on that. All bravado, no sense.

One more glance at Joe showed me that he hadn't moved from the place in his yard. And by then, his porch light was on and Yvette was out there, looking for the cause of all the commotion. Not my business, I thought. *Fire up the lighthouse and show the armada the best place to land, why don't you?*

Sure enough, the white group crossed the tracks, shouting. Me and my group awaited them in the street in front of the field with the big oak. Too often it goes this way. Two teams are told to hate each other, then both sides take the field and fight for some honor they didn't know they needed. I guess it's because they believe what they are told is in a book, but they don't read it. They refuse to find out for themselves. And they deny the lessons their fathers taught them, so they have to relearn the lessons on their own and find that out for themselves, too. It's quite a paradoxical and vicious circle.

Our groups converged and stood just feet apart. It had all the makings of a deadly battle. The screams from both sides were savage and filled with rage. The weapons were brandished in a show of force. The gap between us and them was only a few feet, but the gulf was as wide as they come. More than a stride or two of pavement stood between us. More than a railroad track separated our homes.

Somebody yelled from the white group. "We want justice for our girl!"

"We want justice for our boy that three of your boys followed in a truck and jumped at the filling station!" someone in our group yelled back.

An incident from the previous year. A feeble attempt to make our group the justified aggressors, as if protecting our homes wasn't reason enough to fight. Another step into the dark past that could go on for hours on who hurt who more over the last three hundred years.

Yeah, but what about when you...? The repetitive argument between a couple that was bound for a nasty divorce.

The obvious leader of the white men, a big powerful man covered by a sheet but with a noticeable forearm tattoo, stepped into the small space. He held a machete and motioned toward us in a wide arc with the blade. "We're heading to the rapist's house. Y'all get outta the way now and there won't be no trouble and nobody else will get hurt!"

So, it's our fault if this happens? The mental games between the opposing teams never seemed to stop.

With a deep inhale, I reared my own ax back, deciding his machete blade came close enough to our group to insinuate a clear threat. But an instant before I brought it around and a fierce roar left my lips, Joe walked between our two groups and met the leader in the middle.

"Hold on. Just hold on a minute." He said it like a kid was about to throw a football wrong and he had stopped him midmotion to make a quick correction. I mean to say, he was too quiet and calm for the state of the situation. He went face to face with the leader.

"I said get outta the way! Somebody has to pay for what happened to our girl!" the leader screamed through the sheet. The white group roared in agreement and we roared in response.

"You're right," Joe said without the hostility that surrounded him on all sides. "Someone has to pay, but it'll be the boy who did it. You know he's with the police right now and will probably spend the rest of his life in jail for what he done. None of us here would have it any other way. He did an awful thing and he deserves the punishment that comes with it."

"We want satisfaction!" someone in the white group bellowed.

My group demanded the same, but for a litany of other offenses. Guys behind me started blasting them out, like they were reading bullet points off a chart. The white group fell in with a rebutting diatribe of who did what to whom first.

Joe held up his hands to our group in a call for calm. We stopped fairly quickly and, surprisingly, so did the white group. Maybe we all just realized how dumb it was to be pointing fingers and calling each other names like children on a playground. At any rate, the last thing I heard from either group was a screamed accusation from a white man with a torch, who didn't realize the shouting match was over before he blurted, "You black fellas like to look longingly at our women!"

Longingly, he said. That's the truth and not me paraphrasing. It was an absurd punctuation to an absurd back and forth. The man had a torch and wasn't wearing a sheet. After that little outburst of ridiculosity, I bet he wished he was. Even some of his comrades looked at him like they, like us, were wondering what in the wide world possessed him to say such a thing. Was he shouting down a race he thought inferior or was he writing poetry? He dropped his head in the weird pause that followed.

Joe seemed to ignore it and took advantage of the sudden silence.

"We mourn for that little girl's sake. We got a mother among us who's cryin' for her son and the terrible thing he did. But he's the one responsible. He's the only one who needs to pay."

Another uncovered white man emerged from the crowd. His name was Ron and he was a middle-aged goon known to most of us, since he was one of the more vocal racists that seemed to turn up at high school sporting events. He was a preposterously over-the-top movie caricature before Hollywood started putting such things on film.

"Y'all raised that boy so that makes every one of you culpable!" He lifted a steel pipe over his head. The light from a nearby streetlamp reflected off the metal until it was high enough to reveal that it was a shotgun, and not a pipe after all.

Joe saw it before anyone else. "Put that gun away, ya hear?" he yelled.

The leader turned to Ron then, but Ron jumped forward and jammed the butt of his shotgun forward. It punched Joe hard in the mouth. Joe went down to his knees as a spout of blood erupted from his lips. I dove on Joe to cover him from another attack while Ron was tackled to the ground. Surprisingly, it wasn't anyone in our group that did it. It was the leader of the white group. In his onslaught of Ron, his sheet flew off. I recognized him to be Bill, one of the town's Sheriff deputies. I didn't know him well enough to recognize his voice, but once his sheet was off, I knew his face.

"Why the hell did you bring a gun, Ron? You trying to kill somebody?" Bill seemed angrier at Ron than he had been at our group a minute before. He rained down some haymakers on Ron that left him as bloody as Joe.

I helped Joe to his feet as some guys in the white group pulled Bill off of Ron. I guess everybody is lucky our group was completely dumbfounded because the slightest move toward the white group certainly would have ignited a melee.

Joe held his busted and bloody face. Then, he opened his mouth to let some blood out and that's when I saw that his front tooth was gone.

As Bill and Ron were separated, Ron made a few feeble swings to repair his wounded ego. They weren't even close to landing. "You a son of a bum, Bill!" I might be paraphrasing a bit there. "You with them now?"

"Settle down! Everybody, back off and settle down!" Joe barked. That's when Ron saw the damage he'd done to Joe.

"A tooth ain't all you gonna lose!" he yelled and switched his charge to Joe again. Joe squared his stance, ready to fight, but Bill pushed Ron back.

The white men started yelling once more and our crowd answered. They inched toward each other, but Joe and Bill stayed between both groups. I thought I heard Bill say to Joe, "I didn't know he was armed."

That sent Joe into a rage. It was loud enough to quiet everyone again. "You didn't know he was armed? But pipes and machetes are no big deal, I guess!" He squared off with Bill then, a badger against a bear. "You ought to be ashamed of yourself, Deputy! I thought you was a keeper of the peace?" He pointed a finger in Bill's face, who didn't retaliate in the least. "Now this ain't right and I ain't having it, you hear me?" Then, he jerked his finger around the rest of the group. "Not from you all!" He held his other hand out at our group. "That means everybody!"

"We ain't taking orders from you!" Ron screeched.

"For crying out loud, Ron, shut up!" Bill turned and yelled.

"Don't you think it's time we put an end to their raping ways, Bill? They ain't nothing but a bunch of criminals! All of 'em! They're the ones been asking for a fight!" Ron just wasn't letting it go. Some members of the white group cheered Ron on, fueling him, but it was quite shocking to me that it was only a few of them. Most of the white men stayed silent.

"You're the one's coming at us, in front of our homes, in front of our families!" Joe yelled back. "We heard what that boy did and his people gave him up so he could be dealt with justly. This here," he said as he made a wide arc with his arms. "This ain't justice!"

A covered man in the back of the white crowd must have done something to draw Joe's eye, because Joe turned his attention to him. "You there! Is this what you want or do you want this whole thing to stop so you can be home with your family?"

The man pulled off his sheet and dropped it on the ground. He had tears in his eyes and was obviously the raped girl's father. I found out later his name was Thomas.

"We ain't KKK," he whispered, too choked up to speak loudly.

"I know that. Ain't never been no sheets in this town except on Halloween." Joe, though still riled and flooded with adrenaline, had somehow brought his voice back down to a sympathetic tone. "Your family needs you now. Your daughter does, now more than ever. I'm sorry that these men made you feel like you had to be here instead of at home with her."

Bill waved Thomas off. "Go on home, Tom. This was a mistake." He spoke low and with unmistakable shame. Thomas had already started walking back toward the tracks.

Good ol' Ron made sure his beef wasn't forgotten. "We ain't done here!" At some point, he'd retrieved his gun from whoever had it and rushed Joe.

Like a striking rattlesnake, Joe reached out, grabbed the barrel and ripped it cleanly from Ron's hands. He spun the shotgun, smooth as silk, and had the business end in Ron's face before Ron or Bill or anyone else could react. Ron retreated behind Bill like the coward he was. Bill didn't even try to intervene. To be honest, I think he took a small side-step, as if to give Joe a clear path, but stopped himself in the moment. Joe lowered the barrel so that he wasn't pointing it at Bill and rapidly jacked the shells from it until it was empty.

Ron, with Bill between him and Joe, protested the turn of events. "He's got my gun, Bill!"

"It's a nice gun, too. Believe I'll keep it," Joe snapped.

Bill nodded. "Fair enough. Ron, shut your pie-hole and go home." Bill looked beyond Joe to me and the rest of our group. "We're sorry, guys. We really are. We just let ourselves get a little..." He trailed off, maybe not knowing what else to say.

Ron was well away from both groups before he chimed in again, "You don't speak for me, Bill!" He pointed at Joe. "You'll get yours, every one of you! Another night!" He waved to a few guys in his group. "Y'all coming or what?"

The three or four other guys scampered after him. For the record, Ron never gave Joe 'his' or us 'ours' like he promised, but we knew he wouldn't. In fact, I'm fairly certain I never heard his mouth again at another sporting event.

Bill watched the small group of milksops cross the tracks on their retreat home. He looked at those who stayed. "No more sheets, men."

Those remaining guys removed their sheets and let them fall to the ground. Me and my group of Doreen Street neighbors stood wide-eyed and amazed. Joe spit blood on the ground and wiped his mouth again. "Sorry about your tooth," Bill said.

"Anybody know a good dentist?" Joe asked so everyone could hear.

For the first time, there was a hint of laughter as Bill said, "He just left."

There was a pronounced pause again. Both sides were waiting for a sign from the heavens to let us all know it was the right time to turn around and walk away. It came in the form of Yvette's voice from her porch.

"Y'all get those good linens outta that dirt!" she beckoned. "Soiling your wives' tablecloths and bedsheets like that! They gonna have your hides!"

Everyone looked over and saw Yvette standing on the steps of the porch, hands on her hips, just as sassy as ever.

"Best do as she says, fellas," Joe shrugged. "Trust me."

The white men picked up their sheets. One by one, they turned and walked away. Our guys did, too. Bill stayed and looked hard at Joe for a moment longer. Joe put the end of the shotgun in the ground and leaned on it, like a crutch.

"How'd you know Tom was that girl's dad?" Bill finally asked. "He was covered, same as the rest of us."

"Ain't nothing can shroud a broken heart as big as his," Joe answered. He turned and put his arm on my shoulder. His hand was heavy as he immediately put whatever weight wasn't on the shotgun on me, as if he was about to fall.

I steadied him without looking like I was. Joe was a proud man, and though I could tell he was hurting, I don't think Bill could. Thankfully, Bill turned and left. As he followed the other men toward the tracks, though, he gave a single look back at Joe. And he gave the slightest of nods.

Later that year, on the 31st of October, I was walking over to Joe's. All manner of trick-or-treating goblins and ghouls were running up and down the street and I was going to join Joe for a beer while Yvette passed out candy. I stopped on the sidewalk when I saw Bill, his tattoo stretched across his cantaloupe-sized forearm, standing on Joe's porch. Next to him was a small kid (his 6-year-old son), covered in a sheet to look like a ghost.

Bill knocked on Joe's door. The little ghost called out "Trick or treat!"

The ghost held up a bag for candy as the front door swung open and Joe stepped out. Now, I thought the ghost thing was in pretty bad taste, and I was stomping into Joe's yard to say so when Joe let out a hearty laugh, the wide gap in his teeth exposed for all to see. Joe dropped a generous handful of candy into the little ghost's bag. Bill shook Joe's hand and placed his other hand on Joe's arm, a genuine gesture just short of a hug.

"Thank you, sir," I heard Bill say. Now, that was a rare thing for a white man to say to a black man back then, so I stopped my charge at the bottom of the steps.

"Of course," Joe said. "Anyone willing to dress up so nice as him gets lots of candy." Joe offered Bill a chocolate bar. It was

Bill's turn to laugh then. Bill took the bar and reached in his front pocket.

"I got something for you." He handed Joe a slender box of shotgun shells.

When they turned and left, Bill smiled and nodded at me. The little boy under the sheet looked up at me and said, "He gives good candy, but you gotta dress up."

I went up and stood next to Joe and watched them go back over the tracks. Joe's house was the one house they went to in our neighborhood.

"That was a weird thing for him to do," I said to Joe.

Joe just shrugged. "I think he was trying to make a joke of it. Kind of his way of apologizing maybe."

I think Joe was right because for the next six or seven years, Bill would bring that kid to Joe's on Halloween. Joe would give the kid a bunch of candy and Bill a chocolate bar. Bill would give Joe shotgun shells. The handshakes eventually became hugs. After a few years, the boy didn't think it was fun anymore, even with the extra candy in his bag, so the Halloween visits stopped. Bill made a point to come by Joe's on his own several times a year, though.

Bill worked his way up in the Sheriff's department and eventually became Sheriff of the county. He always watched out for our neighborhood. If there was any trouble, he and a few of his men always came running. And he and his men always addressed Joe politely, with a 'sir'. Like the 'thank you', that didn't happen in other black neighborhoods in those days. But then again, other black neighborhoods didn't have Joe Moore.

I can't even begin to guess how many nights Joe and I would sit on his porch and rock in those rocking chairs and smoke cigars and sip bourbon. Joe always held a cigar in the gap of the missing tooth. He could wedge it right up in that gap and laugh and carry on without so much as shaking loose the ashes.

I guess Joe was the onliest guy I ever met who could make somebody envy a missing front tooth.

Chapter 10

As with any man, even the best of them, Joe wasn't all saintly wisdom and love as I have so far described. Sometimes, he had a sharp, hustler's edge just as his father-in-law suspected. I was guilty of that, too, but so was everyone around us. We grew up in a place where guppies would be eaten by sharks in a moment. Therefore, we made sure we weren't guppies.

One particular example of such came at our work's annual Christmas party. This wasn't a big-city office party that might immediately come to mind, but an after-work party of just the company's employees. It was right after we clocked out for our last day before Christmas, so we were all still in our work clothes and spouses weren't invited. The boss had cleared the center of the warehouse, and we set up some tables. He sprang for a couple kegs of beer and some barbecue from a local joint and had tuned the radio to a station playing Christmas classics. It was fun to cop a buzz, eat some good brisket, and whoop it up with co-workers. We all looked forward to it every year. However, when alcohol is added to a year's worth of animosity that is bound to build up between a bunch of hard-working, testosterone-fueled men, then there is always going to be a release of pressure.

And smoke. Lots and lots of smoke. When the barbecue was devoured, the cigars, pipes and cigarettes came out. The beer kept flowing though, and any grievance one man had with another roared to the surface. More than a few scuffles broke out.

It was tradition, but it seldom ended in much shedding of blood. A black eye or busted lip or two, but nothing too brutal.

Me and Jackie were a different story. We didn't like each other, and we didn't hide it. In fact, the one thing that kept us from getting at each other full-on all year long was that we had a respectful fear of each other. He wasn't sure he could whip me, nor I him. That didn't stop us from jawing at each other, though. Didn't stop us from making bold predictions of how a fight would go down if it happened. Of course, the claims were usually made by one of us when the other one wasn't around. That didn't stop the chest thumping, but it sure stopped the deed from taking place. Both of us claimed we wanted to throw down. Neither one of us took the final step into the arena.

I guess we would have gone on like that forever, but Joe got kind of tired of the ebb and flow and forced us both to back up our pomposities and macho claims. I was into my third cup of beer when I got word. Joe was grinning like that Cheshire cat on the flip side of that wonderland mirror when he told me.

"What the what?" I said, perfectly content to down libations and avoid all physicality for the rest of the year. "You set up an arm-rassling match between me and Jackie? Come on, Joe! Why, man?"

"I sure did. You guys are always bumping gums at each other, talking 'bout who can whip who. Figured it's 'bout time to shut at least one of you up." Joe was a few beers in too, and he was happy as he could be.

Joe was in his early thirties at the time. His missing tooth had become as much a part of his personality as his electric smile. I was in my mid-thirties and closer to forty than I wanted to admit.

"You seen his arms? He's all swolled up like a stuffed pepper. Got fifty pounds on me at least!" I protested. "In a fight, I'd turn that beefed up weasel on his noggin, but arm-rassling? That's right in his wheelhouse."

"He got ten pounds on you at most. His arms only look bigger than yours because they're so much shorter. He's strong as an ox, but you got that lanky, tendon strength. He called you out, bubba. You can't back down now."

"No, you called us out! Besides, he's won arm-rassling contests! Remember that biker deal up in Daytona? Man, he tore through everybody! I heard he's undefeated!"

"No doubt. No doubt. I guarantee you he's good. But, see, that's better for us. They over there setting the odds up against you. That's really good. We win more money that way." Joe glanced at a circle of men gathering around the table and getting loud.

"I don't know, Joe. I don't like it."

"You just gotta get your head right. You strong. You lean. You mean. You a butt-kickin' machine." Joe started toward the table then. "Now dig deep. Visualize. See yourself putting his arm flat on that table. Once you see it, you believe it, and then you achieve it. That's all there is to it." Joe left me with that poor excuse of a pep talk and took off for the action around the table.

"Hey, man! Wait! Where you going? You got me into this! You at least gotta be in my corner!" I griped, finally accepting it was going to happen.

"They laying down money, son. I gotta get in on it. Just visualize. Visualize. No pain, no gain. Defend your house and one hundred and ten percent and stuff." A shabby pep talk for sure.

"Why you leavin' me, Joe?" I asked. "Come back!"

Joe worked his way into the middle of the group. I could hear him over the other guys' yelling. "Who's holding the money? I got two hundred! Two hundred!"

Money slapped down on the table as the men made their bets. One man was in charge of the odds, and he was taking the job seriously. Of course, they favored Jackie. A little too much if you ask me. Heck, I wasn't no slouch.

I remember hanging my head right then. Maybe it was the beer, but I felt alone. I'd been talking and fantasizing about a showdown with Jackie for years. He had with me, too. We were both about to get the thing we claimed we wanted.

I looked over at him across the warehouse.

He was standing like a boxer in his corner with several guys around him. They were rubbing him down and shaking out his arms and riling him up. They must have been better than Joe at inspirational speech because Jackie was looking right at me with hate in his eyes. The worst part was that his work shirt was off, and he was only wearing a sleeveless undershirt. Good gracious, his arms were huge. And, unlike Joe claimed, they didn't appear much shorter than mine.

I glanced away from Jackie pretty quick. I just felt intimidated, I guess. That had never been a problem for me before, but, man, I really just wanted to pack up and go home and look at this thing another way. In the moment, I even started questioning what it was we didn't like about each other. We'd never really had a start to our feud. If there were cross words or affronts that kicked it off, I couldn't remember them. We'd just decided we didn't like each other some years before and bought into it. I don't know. Thinking about it at the time, I thought there was no reason we couldn't be friends.

The look on his face said the possibility of that happening was pretty non-existent at the moment.

I finished my beer, closed my eyes, and figured I'd better hype myself up if no one else was going to do it. Trying to recall Joe's words, I failed miserably. "See it. See it to achieve it? See it to believe it to…" It was gone. "Aww, man."

I looked for Joe. I didn't see him at first, so I called out. "Joe! Hey, Joe! Where you at?"

A few of the guys broke from the giddy anticipation of our contest to look at me like I was a poor sap bound for execution. I finally spotted Joe sliding up next to Jackie, which I was momentarily thankful for because it made Jackie finally direct those crazed, laser-focused eyes away from me. Then, I realized that was the last place Joe should be.

I'm not much of a lip-reader, but right then, I wished I was. I later got the color commentary on what was said.

"Ain't you on the wrong side?" Jackie asked, confused by Joe's defection to his corner.

"Oh, he's my friend and all, but the smart money is on you. I got two bills in your name, my man," Joe boasted.

"So, you're turning on your friend? Man, that's lowdown and dirty."

"Hey, man, this is business," Joe explained. "I got to protect my paper." About then, Joe put his arm around Jackie and led him away from the others. He was talking fast and low, knowing full well he wouldn't have Jackie's attention for long. "Now, listen here. Don't go taking him lightly. He's all sinewy and stringy, but he's got tendons that are animal-strong, ya hear?"

Jackie laughed at that. "Man, look at me." He popped a double bicep pose that looked like he inserted coconuts under his skin. "Boom. You think I care 'bout his tendons?"

Even Joe was impressed. "Dang, buddy. I get it. You all beefed up and he's built like a squirrel. But that ain't what I'm worried about."

"What'd ya mean?"

"He knows he's gonna lose. That's why I'm betting on you. But look, man, once you get him down, watch out. He's gonna come up with a left hook at your melon right away. This whole thing's just a chance for him to deck you. My advice is be ready to duck. If he hits you, you'll know what I mean by tendon strength. He has a punch like a mule-kick. Trust me, brother."

"You crazy, Joe. He wouldn't be that stupid. In front of the boss man and everything? No way."

"I'm telling ya, brother, he's gonna swing. He's scrappy as all get-out, too. You'll take him at the table, but once he starts slugging, you'll have your hands full."

Jackie looked my way again. I figured I'd better try to intimidate him a little, so I gave him my best steely-eyed leer. I swear I saw a moment of doubt cross his face like a storm front.

Joe was in used-car-salesman mode by then. "Now, don't worry. I'll hold him off as soon as he throws his first punch. Just don't let that sucker shot get ya, though, or its lights out, ya hear? Now let's go do this. And remember, I got my Christmas money on you!" Joe patted Jackie hard on the back and the two walked toward the table in the center of the warehouse.

Jackie's friends circled him again and resumed their pep rally. They were loud enough to hear. I didn't need to read lips.

"You got him, Jackie. He's weak! Weak!"

"Ain't even gonna be a match. Break his arm off at the elbow!"

That got Jackie revved again. He lost that look of doubt I thought I had glimpsed a moment before, and his hate flared once more. He rolled his shoulders and did a few air jabs and uppercuts to get loose.

Now what's shadowboxing got to do with arm-rassling? I thought. *Good for the goose...*

I did some shadowboxing of my own. And, boy, I was fast. I watched that look return to Jackie's eyes. The doubtful one.

About then, I realized I could beat him at arm-rassling fair and square. I had tendon strength after-all, just like Joe said. And I didn't need no one to prop me and gas me up and talk me into believing in myself. I could do it! Bring it on!

I got myself so stoked that I gave a spontaneous battle whoop that echoed through the warehouse. With all eyes suddenly on me, I ran to the circle of men with a new invigoration. I pointed at Jackie and yelled, "Let's go, Mudda Cracka!"

Mudda Cracka, or Mother Cracker without the accent, was a term coined in our workshop years earlier by Migdalia, an office secretary who was born in Mexico. She was an older, very Christian woman and she hated all the cursing she heard from us men. No doubt, there was a lot of the typical foul fare burbling from our mouths throughout our workdays, so she eventually caved and joined in... sort of. Though English was her second language, she recognized most of the ugly curse words and never uttered them, but she began using phrases like we did with lighter substitution words (other words and epithets that she had also heard from us) for the really bad ones. She used Bull Shino a lot. The etiology of that is easy enough. She just used Shinola for the curse word and shortened it. Mo-Jabber, Skeezer, Sugar-foot, Butter Duck, Jitterbug, Slabby Bagger, and Crab-wagon were just a few of her creations. They were so effective in conversation that they worked their way into our lexicon and actually replaced the words they were her stand-ins for. After a few years around her, we became the cleanest talking workshop in the county.

But Mother Cracker was her crowning achievement. She didn't mean anything racial by it. She just started using it in almost every interaction. It caught on among the men, but it only worked if it was said in her signature accent. Before anyone knew it, everybody was calling everybody else *Mudda Cracka.*

"You crazy Mudda Cracka."

"Who taught you to do it that Mudda Crackin' way, son?"

"I don't give a Mudda Crack no how!"

So, I guess it was no surprise that I said that when I did. However, it certainly didn't carry the same impact as the real words, which might have been a better choice given the circumstances.

My short-lived air of crazed intimidation evaporated like steam from a cup of Joe's Colombian Bean. I was still alone. I was still hyped. But now, instead of everyone looking at me like I was dangerous and on the edge of insanity, they burst out laughing.

Well, Sugar-foot.

Everyone gathered around the table. The boss man, who had been leading the betting, stopped to wave Jackie and me into the fray. We took our seats opposite each other.

The boss man held his hands over ours as we brought them together. Jackie locked eyes on me and he gripped me so hard he dang near popped my thumb off.

That pretty much settled it in my mind. Jackie had deltoids like bowling balls and his back muscles looked like wide-open barndoors. Veins coursed through his biceps like a mole had crisscrossed his way under Jackie's skin. There wasn't no way I was beating him on that day.

"Everybody ready?" the boss man yelled. The men around us went crazy with cheers. "You boys ready?" he said to me and Jackie.

Jackie growled something. I just nodded.

Hope you didn't bet too much on me, Joe, I thought. *Or did you bet on him like a turncoat chump?*

"Get ready now!" the boss said, firming his hold over both our hands. The warehouse fell silent with anticipation. "Here we go, boys, here we go! Three, two, one!"

I was thinking, *please don't break my knuckles on the table*, when Jackie did a curious thing. He leaned back. Anyone that knows arm-rassling knows that if they lean back, they open the angle of their arm. I saw that and leaned in, getting my shoulder closer to our locked hands. That put my body weight closer to the action, dang near over it, while Jackie was separating himself from it.

I looked up for a split second and saw Joe right beside me. He was smiling big when he gave me the most subtle of nods that seemed to say, "I racked 'em. Now, you break 'em."

When the boss pulled his hand away, the crowd went bananas and Jackie leaned even further back and away. I got a good jump on him and had his hand halfway to the table in a flash.

Jackie grunted as he tried to get his hand back to upright, but he kept leaning back. He was watching me instead of our hands. He yelled and flexed and did all those dramatic things, but my hand was over his and my shoulder was behind that. I had all my body weight pushing down on his mighty, but too outstretched arm. His muscles yelled out louder than he did. It seemed like we were stuck there, his arm at a 45-degree angle from the table and me on top of it, for a good long while.

He was almost lifting me out of my seat. With much more time, he might have curled me back to square, but I mustered enough speed and power to finish him off. I slammed Jackie's hand to the wood.

I couldn't believe it. Neither could the guys around us. I'd won. The onliest person that wasn't shocked was Jackie. He was too focused on what was supposed to come next. He was leaned back even further by then, hoping to avoid the punch he was expecting. Nothing came, though, because I had no intention of doing such an unsportsmanlike thing.

In retaliation for the attack he had prepared for, and must have happened in his mind, he immediately lunged forward with a wild left cross of his own. Well, then...

Now you're in my wheelhouse, Butter Duck.

I slipped the sloppy punch, then went to work. I whacked Jackie with a few fast, stiff jabs as a warm-up, then introduced him to Mr. Uppercutty and the right-left combo I like to call the Sleepy-Time Twins. All three shots smashed home with precision. Ol' Jackie must have felt like he stepped in front of a string of dump trucks loaded with dancing sugar plums, because that's all he saw from the floor for the next few minutes.

That is how legends are born in a workplace and mine jumped to the top of our mountains of myths. Until the day I retired almost thirty years later, I was the guy who beat Jackie Howard twice in the same night. My left fist became known as "Six Months In A Coma" and my right was called "Sure Death." Maybe I had a little to do with the naming, but the fact remains, nobody messed with me or challenged me after that.

When all of the mayhem that followed eased, and the inordinate amount of drinking that followed the mayhem was still ongoing, Joe collected his winnings and we left the warehouse. He had bet on me, sure enough. Of course, he cut me in on the payout with a more than equitable offering. I was still too thrilled to count it or even care if I got it. Victory was stimulant enough.

"Man, I knew you didn't bet against me," I said as I caressed my right biceps. "How much did my power piston win you?"

Joe flashed a wad of cash that was still pretty fat even after he'd handed a good portion of it to me. "Odds as they were, it's enough to make for a good Christmas! We stopping at the Piggly Wiggly on the way home!"

"I always wondered what Christmas was like at the Rockefeller's," I said, still beaming with pride.

"You had him from the drop, baby," Joe exalted.

"Who wouldn't have, the way he was leaning back, stretching his arm out almost straight?" I mimicked my quick arm move to get over top of him. "I buried his knuckles in the table, didn't I? Outta sight!" I went from reliving the arm-rassling to some shadowboxing. "Then to come up at me with that weak ol' sissy attempt at a haymaker. What was he thinking?"

"I guess some people can't stand losing."

"Boy, I crossed his I's and dotted his T's, didn't I?" I bounced around outside the open door to Joe's truck, still boxing the air. "Sha-kaw. Sha-kaw. That was outta sight!"

We both laughed as we got in. That was a good night. One of the best. I didn't know that Joe had orchestrated my victory at the time, but it didn't change a thing when I finally found out. It just proved his shrewd mind and my forceful physicality were a power combination that could knock out anyone.

We were a dynamic duo and would be for the rest of our lives. At least that's how it felt that night.

Chapter 11

Every dynamic duo like me and Joe has mighty battles in their history. One war isn't enough. They need several. And we had them. I guess that's why I felt compelled to follow up my victory over Jackie by stepping into it with a kangaroo.

Now, Jackie was a tough nut to crack, but the night I squared off with a kangaroo might equal Achilles versus Hector (see, I know they were enemies) or Ali versus Frazier. The sole difference was I always had Joe Moore in my corner and those other chumps didn't.

Not that it helped in this case.

There was a dastardly fad in the 70s and 80s where bars would do anything to get people to come through their doors. One bar in particular was on the coast a bit south of our town. It was a raucous joint and it tried everything to draw a crowd. It was the classically offensive stuff like female bikini mud wrestling and little people tossing and on and on. Looking back, it was all terrible, and honestly, I knew it even then. That place wasn't a bar my core friend group or I went to, but a bunch of guys from work did and that's how we knew about all the shenanigans going on there.

One summer, they set up a boxing ring and brought in a trained kangaroo to fight their patrons. The deal was that a guy and his friends could run up a tab all night, then one of them would get in the ring with the kangaroo and go a few rounds. If the guy got through three two-minute rounds without giving up, the bar would pay their tab. It was a great gimmick that brought in a ton of people. Now, I'm not saying it was right or moral. Clearly, it wasn't. I'm not even going to say it was justifiable for the time, but it happened and I participated in it and there it is.

The kangaroo was undefeated through the summer. Nobody could stay in the ring with this Aussie whirlwind of a pugilist. The guys at work who went to the bar regularly kept the rest of us posted on his winning streak. He even made the local newspaper under the headline 'Kenny the Kangaroo Just Can't Lose'. Had his picture and everything.

One guy at work, a fairly stout dude, had crawled into the ring one night and gotten flattened by Kenny in the second round. He came to work saying nobody in the world could go toe to toe with this ferocious, highly trained beast. My situation with Jackie was still very strong in the collective memory at work, so it was no surprise when the guy pointed at me, the recently declared company top dog, and said, "Not even you, hoss!"

With only a week left in his residency at the bar, I got to thinking I could take on that overgrown opossum. That would be a nice addition to my legend amongst the guys, I figured, so I started talking it up. Now, I've already mentioned how I'd been in some serious rumbles in my time. There was no way I could allow myself to duck a kangaroo after a challenge had been issued. And trust me, a newspaper article and that guy bloviating how Kenny was unbeatable was challenge enough.

Joe was the onliest person to tell me it was a bad idea.

"Look, man, why do you want to go down there to that nasty place and fight a poor animal?" he said after I had told everyone I was going to take on Kenny the next Friday night. "That thing ain't done nothing to you and I guarantee you he doesn't want to be in that ring. Leave it alone, bubba."

"I can't back out now, Joe," I protested, like I didn't have a choice in the matter. "Besides, ain't no billabong of a wallaby in the world can take a solid punch from me." I held up my left fist and shook it. "Six months in a coma, remember?"

"Suit yourself," Joe said as he walked away. "You might be sorry, though."

"Hey," I said. "You're going, right? You'll be there?"

Joe nodded. "Sure, I'll be there. It's probably the dumbest thing you've ever done, but I'll be there. I'm gonna run up a chunky tab too, so if you lose, you gonna have to pay it."

"Not happening, but okay," I laughed. Dumbest thing I'd ever done? Not likely. I was naturally gifted with the talent for doing stupid stuff. Besides, victory was a certainty, I just knew it. I had a plan, after all.

That Friday night, I showed up at the crowded bar with five guys in tow, one of them being Joe. I got a lay of the land really quick. Kenny wasn't in the ring yet. For prefight festivities, they were lacing up gloves on two guys at a time and letting them go at it. Whoever wanted to get in there and slug it out was welcome to climb through the ropes. That helped build a high energy in the place. And believe me, when I say that place was popping, it was popping. Dudes that had issues with each other went at it. Friends went at it. It was one punch-fest after another and the crowd loved it. The bar was bursting at the seams. Liquor and beer flowed like I have never seen.

While all this was going on, the bar officials started taking names of would-be fighters for Kenny later in the night. I put my name in the hat and was selected as Kenny's sixth and final opponent of the card. I signed the waiver put before me without reading it. Wasn't no need. I was gonna whip Kenny good.

Me and my boys opened a tab and off we went. They drank like fish, but I didn't. And that was the main part of my plan. This wasn't about pleasure for me. This was a business trip. I'd figured that the offer to pay the tab was how the bar guaranteed Kenny would win. Guys would take advantage of the open tab and drink way too much for several hours. By the time they got into the ring, those guys were stumbling and bumbling and seeing double. Kenny carved them up with sharp jabs and stiff uppercuts.

The night wore on and Kenny took to the squared circle amid wild, crazed applause from the insane crowd. He dispatched the first five opponents with relative ease. In between each fight, Kenny would go in the back, and they would toss out two drunk schmucks to throw hands and keep the crowd rabid with anticipation. They drug it out for hours, but the announcer was good. He kept the energy and the bloodlust high.

When it was my turn, it was getting late, and I was stone-cold sober. I'd studied Kenny and his repetitive fighting style in the bouts preceding mine. I had him and I knew it. It was going to be a walk in the park. Joe, who had drunk some, but not as much as the other guys in my crew, took his place by my side. He helped me put on the gloves they'd given me, which were sopping wet with the previous fighters' liquor sweat.

By then, Joe was thinking like me. He knew I could take that kangaroo with relative ease.

"Just dance around and pop him a few times. Don't hurt the poor little fella. Go three rounds so they'll pay our bill and we can get out of here."

I nodded. "You got it," I said, but I knew I wasn't going to do that. I was gonna knock that varmint out. And fast, too.

Once I was laced up and in the ring, and the announcer had the crowd in a suitable alcohol-fueled lather for the final fight of the evening, Kenny was brought back out by his handlers. He was smaller than he had appeared from my perspective outside the ring, and I doubted the top of his head would have reached my chest if he stood on his tippy toes, assuming kangaroos had tippy toes. He was actually pretty cute and was wearing adorable little leather gloves. They were smeared with the slobber from his previous five victims, but there was no blood. I knew he'd knocked out the other guys because they were stewed like prunes. He couldn't even hit hard enough to cut skin.

Kenny bounced up and down through the raucous introductions and he never really looked at me, even though I was staring him down. Kind of the reverse of what happened between me and Jackie not too long before. For a moment, I felt sorry for him. Maybe Joe was right. Maybe I should've had mercy on him.

But, alas, I did not.

The crowd was screaming like crazy. I was feeling energized and ready. And, most importantly, I was clear-headed and fresh. Kenny had already fought five times. He was disinterested and inattentive to the matter at hand.

With the introductions over, Joe leaned across the rope toward me and said, "Go easy, bubba. Go easy. Poor critter ought to be in a zoo. Not here."

I nodded, they rang the bell, and me and Kenny met in the middle of the ring. I towered over him. He made some futile jabs, but I dodged them easily. He upper-cutted, but I leaned back, and he missed with those, too.

I circled him for most of the round, sizing him up. He bounced on his haunches to keep facing me, but he didn't advance. He just kept poking the air with his little gloves. His swings were feeble and easy to slip. Toward the end of the first two minutes, I decided to strike. As if it was choreographed, I stopped in the middle of the ring. Kenny did, too. He just stood there facing me, bouncing lightly on his back feet.

For my first punch of the night, I went with the Widowmaker. I didn't even set him up with jabs. Nope, I went right for the knockout. I reared back and threw a mighty right cross. It connected solidly, right in Kenny's snout. And let me just say, it was a powerful shot. His eyes crossed and I practically saw little birds tweeting around his head. He was out on his feet. In what seemed like slow motion, he started going backwards. I raised my hands over my head in victory, easy though it was.

Now, here's the problem. I had never seen a kangaroo in real life before that night. I had never watched one fight in the wild. Had I done so, I would have backed away because, it turns out, a wild animal can be taught to do certain tasks, like boxing. However, the second it is severely threatened or hurt, it reverts back to its true nature. I didn't know that Kenny wasn't really knocked out. I thought I'd hit him so hard that he was horizontal in mid-air and levitating there like in a cartoon. I expected him to stay there a second or two, then fall flat to his back when gravity kicked in. What I didn't see was that his tail was curved under him like a runner on a rocking chair. He wasn't levitating. He was going slowly backwards on his long, strong, spring-loaded tail, like he was going into a backswing for a strikeout fastball pitch.

Needless to say, I was watching his hands and waiting for him to drop to his back on the canvas. Instead, he rocked back and then, ten times faster than he went backwards, he came up, and he used his tail to launch him forward. He kicked me with both feet right square in the chest and it might as well have been a head-on collision with a charging Clydesdale or a Mack truck or the express train. The blast sent me all the way across the ring and through the ropes. I heard my ribs crack. And before I even hit the floor outside the ring, I knew I was going to die.

Turns out, I almost did. I had what is called 'flail chest', which is what happens when there are multiple breaks in the rib cage. My lungs collapsed and filled with blood. I needed immediate medical intervention. My last sight before I passed out was of Joe leaning over me. Behind him, I saw Kenny in the ring, looking down at me. I swear he smiled. What a conceited little stinker he turned out to be.

I spent a week in a coma. I guess it would have been hilariously ironic if it was six months. When I finally woke up and they took out my breathing tube, who was at my side? Joe, of course. And Yvette.

"I told you not to mess with that poor kangaroo," he said with a shake of his head.

"What do I owe you for the tab?" was all I could manage to croak out since my throat was sore from the tube and my chest hurt something awful.

"Nothing. We left in an ambulance so fast, we never had a chance to settle our bill."

Yvette started laughing then. "Tell him what you did, Joe."

Joe started to speak, but Yvette jumped in before he could say a thing. I'd found out later she'd drank coffee while holding vigil at my bedside. Lots and lots of coffee. She was wired.

"He rented a real nice suit and went back to the bar and talked to the owner. The owner thought Joe was your lawyer!"

"I never implied I was," Joe interjected. "What he inferred is his problem."

"Yeah, well, he got the owner of that joint to cover your tab, your hospital bills, and he also cut you a check for five thousand dollars for all the work you're missing," Yvette rattled. "So long as nobody calls the TV news or the newspapers."

"And Kenny was relocated to a zoo up in Atlanta," Joe added, his proudest accomplishment of the whole situation, it seemed. "From what I hear, he loves it there. Lots of room to hop around. Making friends left and right."

It was a lot to take in. Somehow Joe had set everything straight for me while I was pulling a Rip Van Winkle.

"Stupid opossum," I rasped, unable to say much more.

"I talked to a real lawyer, and he said Joe did you better than he could've. Said you signed a waiver that would have made it hard to sue the bar," Yvette informed me. "Joe's threats to go to the press did the trick."

"The waiver didn't mention that ol' Kenny might karate-cize you with a double front kick. Boy, he booted you through the uprights, I'll tell you that." Joe was laughing by then. I chuckled too, but it really hurt my chest too much so I stopped. "Say, maybe while you're laid up, we can learn to play chess," Joe said when he saw how laughing made me miserable.

"Good idea!" Yvette chimed in. "Y'all need to slow down with your trifling antics anyway."

I nodded, but that hurt my throat. "Let's do it," I ribbited.

I was in that hospital bed for two more months. Joe was by my side for a good part of it. We watched a lot of baseball and football and basketball and more than our share of Family Feud, but we never did learn to play that game.

About a year later, Joe drove me to the Atlanta Zoo. I made peace with a certain marsupial, and I bought me and Joe spiffy new ball caps in the gift shop.

Chapter 12

A man has many faces, many facets, that are shown to the public and likewise hidden from it at different times in his life. Men have family faces, and work faces, church faces and faces they put on when they're around just the guys. We can be kings, knights, soldiers, cowboys, and pirates depending on what we're up to and who's watching.

Joe was no different. He might be the best example of it, truthfully.

He was brave, wily, slick, genuine, a guy that would give you everything he had if you needed it. He was also, as I alluded already, deathly afraid of thunderstorms.

He didn't think it was funny, but I ribbed him about it every chance I got. It was an irrational fear if you ask me, one reserved for little kids and dogs. He'd always been that way though, and he'd learned to live with it and cope as best he could.

The guys at work didn't know about it because he covered it up pretty well. When a storm rolled through during work hours, he got edgy and nervous, but he usually excused himself for one reason or another and dealt with his fear in a place where he could be alone.

He wasn't so covert at home. In fact, Yvette had had just about all she could handle of his phobia, and she wasn't too shy about hiding it.

Every time Joe was home and a storm rolled through, he bolted to his room. Yvette would undoubtedly find him in their walk-in closet. Joe would be huddled on the floor, arms wrapped around his knees, rocking back and forth, shaking, eyes wide with abject fright.

Yvette would just stand there with her hands on her hips, as unsympathetic as they come, even as the windows would light up with each strike of lightning and the walls would rattle with each crash of thunder.

"For crying out loud, Joe, are you sitting on my shoes again?"

Joe would be catatonic. She would just slam the door and start away. "Grown man trembling like that over a storm! Shameful! Scandalous and scurrilous and shameful!"

He'd stay until the storm passed. Yvette wouldn't say anything when he finally emerged, but every storm had a way of eroding things. I think Joe was always afraid she had lost a little bit of respect for him as a man with every duck and run he gave into. He always got quiet and hung his head for a while afterward, and during the summer in Central Florida, that equals a lot of regret.

Chapter 13

I still had sand in my britches. So much so that if I moved too fast, I could feel the grit grinding deep in my gears. If I were to run for any reason, I probably would have sawed myself in half.

Willie was by my side. Joe was still miffed that I had let him laugh so hard. I brushed myself off as best I could. Then, I shook my pants legs to get any free-floating sand out. I looked down at Willie. He watched me closely, smiled, then did the same with his little drawers.

How cute can one kid be?

"Keep an eye on Willie and Mister Jagged Man," Joe huffed. "I'm gonna load the smoker."

I gave him a playful salute. "Aye aye, Caption," I said. I always had confused Caption and Captain. Good thing I wasn't a military man anymore. Sculptor and sculpture were two other ones I mixed up. I looked down the road, but didn't immediately see the Stranger. Willie went back into the sandbox, so I ambled up the steps to the porch.

The sculpture created a beautiful sculptor. Honestly, those were easy to confuse.

It couldn't have been long, maybe ten minutes, before Joe came back out the front door, wiping his hands on a rag. I was in the rocker by then, watching Willie and lost in my own thoughts.

"That smoke is getting right," Joe said. Suddenly, he spotted the Stranger in front of Felicia's house. The Stranger was cupping his hands around his face and staring through Willie's bedroom window.

Joe rushed to the porch railing, yelling. "Hey! Hey! Get away from that house, ya hear? You got no business being there! Go on! Get outta that yard!"

I was shocked to see him there, since I had been keeping an eye out every now and again. "Whoa, how'd he get there so fast? He was way on down the road a second ago. I've been watching him." I got up and joined Joe in chastising the man. "Go on! Get away from there!" I was probably a little too defensive when I turned to Joe. "I swear it, Joe, I just looked at him and he was way over on the other side of my house. Way on the other side."

Joe paid me no mind and kept yelling across the yard. "You leave that house alone!"

The Stranger ignored Joe and started blowing through pursed lips, making a weird gushing noise. Then, he loped out of the yard, all twisty and turny, and stopped on the sidewalk beside the power pole in front of Felicia's house.

Joe turned his attention to Willie down below. "Willie. C'mon up here, son. Come see Granddaddy."

Willie looked up from the sandbox at Joe, just as the Stranger's lips reshaped. He blew again and he made a loud whistle. It drew Willie's attention. He stood, locked on the man, and stepped out of the sandbox. Joe hurried down the stairs.

"No, no! Come here, boy. Don't you bother with that man!"

The Stranger hit another whistle. Willie trotted straight for him. Joe dashed after Willie.

"Willie!" Joe hollered. "Stop! Come here!"

On the sidewalk in front of Felicia's house, Willie ran up to the Stranger, aiming his sweet smile up at him. The Stranger had a vacant expression and moved side to side in a rocking motion. He was about to place his palm on Willie's head when Joe sprinted up and intervened.

"Don't you think about touching that boy, ya hear?"

The Stranger's eyes widened as Joe pulled Willie back by the arm, out of his reach. I rushed to Joe's side.

"Go on, get out of here!" I said, waving him off.

Joe's eyes stayed on the Stranger as he bent down and picked Willie up. Willie clung to Joe like a koala bear. The Stranger stopped rocking then and became extremely still. He met Joe's stare with dark, vacant eyes. There was an odd smile beneath the Stranger's sharp nose. His eyes were lifeless. For a moment, there seemed to be a violent swirl in them, as if they were filled with a tempestuous, syrupy liquid.

The sight of the man caused Joe to take a big step back, still nestling Willie tightly in his arms. The Stranger began to hiss ever so low. I could barely hear it and I was right there.

"Wh- what?" Joe stuttered. "What did you just say?" His voice was panic-stricken. Other than the hiss, I hadn't heard anything remotely close to words coming from the Stranger.

Just like that, Joe lunged for him, but I grabbed Joe's arm and held him back because he still had Willie. I stepped between the Stranger and Joe.

"Time for you to leave," I growled as menacingly as I could.

The Stranger began blowing through pursed lips again but made no whistle or hiss. Just the gushing. He reached out to the power pole that was beside him and placed his palm flat on it without looking. With his other hand, he reached around me, still trying to touch the boy. Joe pulled him back.

The Stranger's finger grazed Willie's cheek as I pushed his arm down and away. I balled my hands into fists. "Son, you 'bout to find out."

The Stranger slipped a jagged grin and continued hissing.

Joe was panicked again when he yelled, "Don't you say that! Don't you dare say that!" He recoiled further away with Willie.

The Stranger pooched his lips, then he hit that terrible, shrill whistle once more. He rocked side to side and back and forth for a moment before loping and skipping away from us. There was an arrogant satisfaction in his flouncy swagger. He didn't look at anything else as he crossed Doreen Street and headed in the direction of the old oak tree in the field.

"What do you want me to do, Joe? What do you think we should do?" I said as I turned to Joe.

"My phone is in the house," Joe replied. His face was blanched, and he looked like he had seen a horrible car crash. "He touched Willie. He threatened him. Call the police."

I started back for the house, watching the Stranger as I went. Joe stayed on the sidewalk behind me, still holding the boy. He kept watching the Stranger like me. I could hear Willie starting to squirm and whine in Joe's arms.

I climbed Joe's porch stairs. The Stranger was under the canopy of the oak. I turned to find the door handle and flung the door open. I gave a final glance back at the tree. The Stranger was gone. The tree's leaves rustled a bit, but he was nowhere to be seen.

"Where'd he go?" I called back to Joe.

His reply was urgent. "Just go call!"

I didn't find his cell anywhere right away, so I called '911' from his house phone. From its mount on the wall, I could see through the window to the outside. Joe was still on the sidewalk, but he was shaking so bad that he had to set Willie down before he dropped him.

After I'd made the call, I wandered from Joe's yard into the street. I looked toward the oak tree, then back at Joe. He was exhausted in his rocker, holding Willie on his lap. I went into the field and stood beneath the oak and looked up into its branches. The air was still and stagnant. The shade of the canopy offered no reprieve from the heat.

"See anything?" Joe called out to me.

I looked back then and saw that Joe and Willie had walked out to the street and were holding hands on the centerline.

"Nah," I called back. "He didn't leave anything. Not even a footprint that I can see."

"Don't muck it up in there. The cops might want to see for themselves."

I walked back and joined them. Willie was reaching up toward Joe, motioning for him to pick him up again.

"Your legs tired already? Huh?" Joe asked the boy. He nodded. Joe hefted him into his arms and Willie pointed at the playground next to Joe's house.

"Just for a minute. And only if you promise not to run up to strangers again."

I followed them across the street to the playground. Joe put the boy in a swing, pulled him back and got the boy swinging. I found a seat on a nearby bench.

"Whew," I said as I mopped my brow. "Don't tell me it's still too early for Ol' Red?"

Joe didn't answer. It wasn't like us to go so long without talking, and I was getting a bit uncomfortable with the lapse in conversation.

"Hey, did you ever tell Willie about the showdown you had here?" Joe kept pushing Willie without looking at me. "Right over there, I believe." I pointed toward the area of the park next to Joe's yard. "Yes sir. A real high noon showdown if I ever saw one." The memory made me chuckle. "Boy howdy, was he a punk or what? I thought for sure you was gonna deck him. You'd woulda been right to do it, too."

Joe finally gave a crooked smile. "Imagine how things might be now if I had."

I just shook my head and laughed to myself. "Now that was something. Talk about a crossroads in life. That was really something."

It was something, indeed.

Chapter 14

I reckon I mentioned all that other stuff about Joe to tell this part of his story. It has to be clear what kind of man Joe was to fully understand his relationship with that rascal Isaac. The story of his meeting with his Father-in-Law, the way he talked down that mob at the tracks, and his craftiness in dealing with Jackie and Kenny the kangaroo's greedy owner are all requisite stories to fully understand the most important one.

Isaac was a turd of the highest order and there was no two ways around it. I could dig deep in my vocabulary and describe his character with some flourish, but why bother? That's the best word for him, plain and simple.

Our first meaningful interaction with him started when he and a group of five other boys, all about 10 or 11 years old, walked by in the street. They were bouncing a few basketballs between them.

Now, most of the boys living in our neighborhood admired Joe because he was such a fixture on the street and he didn't take much guff from any of them. They would always treat him cordially and try to be on their best behavior when he was around. I asked him once why he thought they gave him such respect and no one else (meaning me). He said it was because he had a beautiful daughter and they all wanted to get in good with him. I think there was more to it than that. Of course, the respect thing only applied when he was around. When he wasn't, they acted the fool. To me, they were all little rapscallions all the time.

On this particular Saturday, those boys were headed to the playground. It had a basketball court back then. That court was eventually removed after it fell into a bad state of disrepair. In those days though, it was a magnet for the area's ruffians.

When they went in front of Joe's house, all the boys except one waved at Joe. He was close to 50 then. I was in the chair beside him, but those boys didn't pay me no mind at all. We'd been fishing that morning and had the smoker fired up in the backyard to make up a batch of smoked mullet. We were drinking iced tea and taking five.

The boys called out in unison. "Hey, Mister Moore." They always called him Mister Moore. All except Isaac. He was the tallest of the boys and he was smoking a cigarette and not even trying to hide it. He didn't acknowledge Joe in any way.

Once at the playground, Isaac and the other boys played basketball for a while. They abandoned their game pretty quick though (maybe it was all those cigarettes) and took to hanging around the slide, talking, jiving, and cursing, all of which was way too loud.

Several children were playing on the swings and teeter-totters nearby and their mothers were standing close. The two women were uneasy about the language. One of the mothers approached the loud teens.

"You boys stop that loud cussing and go on from that slide. Our kids wanna play."

I already mentioned that the boys had cesspool mouths and what poured out of Isaac's mouth in reply was more than enough to prove it. I also mentioned that a good Christian secretary from work made up her own words to replace the vile ones that surrounded her every day. I believe this would be a good time to do the same. From here on out, I'll tell the story like Migdalia might have.

"Step off with your slabby-baggin' self," Isaac burst out. "We got here first. Take them scatty brats to some other park!"

"Somebody ought to scrub your tongue with soap!" the mother reprimanded him.

Well, Isaac was as gross as he was vile. He just stuck out his tongue suggestively. "Have at it," he said.

Disgusted and flabbergasted, both mothers gathered her kids. "Come on, kids! We're going home!"

Me and Joe were still on the porch and watched the whole exchange. By the time Isaac had wagged that nasty tongue of his, Joe was already at the base of his steps and calling out to the group of boys, who had trouble hearing him because they were laughing at Isaac so hard.

"Hey! Boys! Get over here!" Joe demanded.

Finally, the boys turned. Their faces dropped when they realized Joe had seen everything, except of course for Isaac. That boy didn't give two hoots.

"What's the matter with you?" Joe barked while he was pounding toward the playground with heavy feet. He stopped about where the playground and his yard met.

One of the boys was quick to cave and he turned as mild-mannered as he could be. "We was just hanging out, Mister Moore."

The women with the kids hadn't left yet, so they stood by, watching closely.

"We were just joking around. They can have the slide," another boy said, suddenly sheepish.

Isaac wasn't about to relent. "Hey, yo! What's the problem? You the neighborhood watch or something?" He was doing that sideways, two-fingered point thing, like his hand was a pistol. It came off super-aggressive.

"You bet I am, son, and I don't like what I see." Joe was keeping his cool.

"Son? What'd you think you see, jitterbug?"

"You acting like street trash in front of those young 'uns. Don't let me hear that garbage come outta your mouth again, understand? Where's your decency, boy?"

Isaac started toward Joe then, with his chest puffed and arms held out from his sides like he had barn door back muscles like Jackie did back in the day. He didn't, though. It was just posture and bravado. He was a skinny twerp. A mere banty rooster.

"What we done to you, mo-jabber? Why don't you mind your own skeezin' business?"

"You're cursing at innocent mothers and kids and you think it ain't none of my business?" Joe crossed his arms. "You're steps from my house. That talk don't fly around here."

One of the boys walked up behind Isaac and nudged his arm. "C'mon, Isaac. Let's motor."

"Naw, man. I wanna hear what he gonna do if we stick around." Isaac crossed his arms, too.

By then, I'd had enough. "Isaac!" I yelled and started down from the porch.

Isaac wasn't giving an inch and didn't seem a bit fazed by my approach. "All you do is preach at us every day and go smoking up the neighborhood with that stinking fish every night! I'm tired of you standing on that porch and nobbling our scobs when you can't do nothing to us! You can't do nothing period!"

I was by Joe's side then. "Why you little...! No court in the land will blame me!" I leapt at him, but Joe put out his hand to stop me. Joe just stayed calm and smirked confidently at Isaac.

"I can do anything you can," he said.

Isaac scoffed and waved Joe off. He turned to his friends and laughed. "Oh, okay! You can't do nothing like me!"

"I said it, so I meant it. I can do anything you can," Joe said. Isaac looked at him with his head cocked. "You show me something right here, right now, and if I can't do it, then I'll leave you alone."

I nudged Joe then and leaned close. "Tread lightly, man. I've seen him dunk." In all our time together, which included many a pick-up basketball game, I'd never seen Joe come close to dunking a ball. I'd never even seen him within a foot of the rim.

Of course, Isaac heard me because my whisper voice is about as quiet as my knees popping. Which is to say, it ain't.

"Yeah, that's right. I can dunk and you sure as shino can't do that," he bragged.

"Try me," Joe said. His eyes were on fire right then. So much so that I started to believe he might be able to dunk a ball and he had been playing a long con on me for thirty years for just such an occasion as this.

His intense stare worked because Isaac took a step back. "So, if I dunk a ball and you don't, then you gotta quit cooking that fish and telling us what to do?"

Joe just nodded. "And what do I have to do if you win?"

"Easy. Just quit cursing and smoking those cigarettes. And start acting like a respectable human being."

"You gonna make me go to church every Sunday, too?" Isaac quipped. He laughed again. His friends didn't. Neither did the mothers and their kids. All eyes were on Joe and Isaac. Everything else was in the background.

"Dunk and find out." Joe said it so doubtlessly that I imagined, in that moment, he was capable of leaping over the net, the backboard, everything.

One of the boys tossed Isaac the ball, but he just dribbled a few times and tossed it back.

"Anything I can do?" Isaac said for reassurance. Joe nodded. "Just remember, you picked this fight."

Isaac walked away from the group. He stopped, stood still for a second, then he did a perfect backflip. He stuck the landing, too. His posse fell all over each other, jeering and doing that whole bit. The mothers gasped.

Me? Well, I was always impressed by acrobatics, so I found myself clapping before I caught myself and stopped. I leaned toward Joe and said in my signature whisper-yell, "Dang, that was good."

"You get your chicken-legged old jibbit to do that and I'll crump your mamby," Isaac sneered.

Joe shook his head in amazement. "How 'bout that? Always loved watching people do backflips."

"This ain't a 'watching' contest," Isaac smirked. "You gonna do one or you just gonna stand there with your toothless mouth flapped open?"

Man, he had a way of making me want to pop him good.

The mothers chimed in from the sidelines. "Oh, Joe, don't even..." said one.

"We're leaving, Joe. It's all good," said the other.

Joe just chuckled. "Honestly, Isaac, I was hoping you might just rub your belly and pat your head or make those pooty noises with your armpit. I didn't know you could do gymnastics."

"Yeah, that's what I thought. It'll be nice to finally have some peace 'n quiet 'round here. Be able to breathe some no-fish-stinking air for a change." Isaac flipped Joe off then and turned to walk back toward his friends, who were suddenly quite unconcerned with showing Joe respect. "See ya later, Old Joe!" He really put emphasis on the 'Old' part.

I was kind of surprised when Joe kept talking. "Hold on, now! I just said you did really good. Didn't say I was conceding defeat."

"What?" Isaac shot back. "Look at your ragged old self. You can't do no backflip."

"You're right about that. Least I can't do 'em yet. Give me a little time though and I will."

"Time?"

"Yep. Three weeks. That's what I need. Three weeks and I'll match you flip for flip."

"You said--" Isaac started, but Joe interrupted him.

"I said anything you could do, I could do. I didn't say nothing 'bout me doing it right now. I'm an old man. You gotta give me a little bit of leeway on something like a backflip."

"Oh, come on, man! A loophole? Never figured you to be that lame."

"Not a loophole. A time allowance for my age. I'll accept the terms of your challenge, but you got to give me three weeks to train."

"Man, you ain't never gonna do no backflip. Not in your lifetime."

"Don't need a lifetime, Isaac. Just three weeks. We got a deal?"

"No fish smoking and riding our backs until that day then?" Isaac asked. Joe reached out his hand. Isaac gave it a quick shake. "Catch you in three weeks, crab wagon!" he laughed.

The boys walked off, laughing and shaking their heads. Joe and I watched them go. Even the mothers shook their heads and sauntered off. I think they thought it was over and Joe had cowered without actually admitting it. I think they thought they'd lost the slide for good.

"I thought you was gonna give that boy the 'what for'. You did good, though. Showed more restraint than I coulda," I said. I had the same feeling as I assumed the mothers had. I was hoping to smooth the edges of the situation for Joe's ego's sake.

Joe stood silent, still watching the boys strut down the street. The awkward silence got the best of me yet again.

"You know, three weeks ain't long." Joe didn't answer. "You ever even tried doing one of them whoopty-doos?"

That got Joe talking. "I know what I'm doing, so don't say another word."

"Yeah, but you got that bum knee and that nerve deal in your neck. And the only athletics you ever done was football. And that was thirty..."

"Dang it, man, I said don't say another word! Don't you know what that means? It don't mean talk a bunch!"

"You was the punter, wasn't ya? I used to see you practicing with the junior varsity. They said you were too short., didn't they? How short is too short to be a punter on a JV team?"

Joe huffed, turned, and walked toward his house.

"Course I was leading the varsity team as an all-state wideout, but, you know, I looked over at that other field on occasion."

Joe waved me off with a harsh "Go on home, bubba!"

"I'm kinda glad he didn't dunk, aren't you?" Finally, the thing I was fishing for occurred.

Joe smiled.

Chapter 15

That afternoon, good to his word to Isaac, but much to my dismay, Joe extinguished the fire in the smoker. Since Joe didn't have a porch on the backside of the house, I was drinking more iced tea on his back steps. Joe stood on the upper rung of a ladder and arranged a network of pulleys to a limb of a back-yard oak. I was watching him, quite amused, when Yvette flung the screen door and looked out with her arms crossed.

"Hey baby," Joe said.

"Don't you 'hey baby' me! What do you think you're doing?" she demanded.

"It's a training mechanism I invented. Figure I'll practice with these pulleys, then gradually reduce the support as I get better. Before you know it, I'll be popping out the backflips like a pro-fessional." Poor Joe said it like he thought Yvette might actually believe it.

"Don't tell me you're serious about that nonsense with that demon-seed!"

"'Course I'm serious. Wouldn't be worth a snot if I wasn't."

Yvette brushed past me on her way down into the yard. "Aside from paralyzing yourself, explain to me what you think this is going to accomplish?"

Joe stopped his work and thought for a moment. "I think I'll do a backflip for starters. Then Isaac will honor his word and stop smoking and cursing. Could end up making him a better person in the long run."

"My foot, Joe. That boy ain't no good. His daddy wasn't no good and neither was his granddaddy. Isaac's gonna end up in jail just like the both of 'em. It's too thick in his blood and there's no use trying to change that."

Joe came down the ladder and stood in front of Yvette. "And it's that kind of thinking that'll make him that way. He just needs help avoiding that path everybody seems so determined to send him down."

"And you think a backflip will do that?"

"It might break a link in the chain."

Yvette wasn't having it. "Might break your neck." She looked back at me. "He might break his neck before he breaks a link in any chains."

I nodded. What else could I do?

"I know some of his teachers. Every one of 'em says he's smart as any kid they've ever taught. He just needs to apply himself." Joe was still pleading his case.

"Oh, so you've taken to spying on him?"

"Not today, obviously, but I've heard things about him the last few years. Besides, I gotta know who I'm risking my neck for," Joe smiled.

"And what if a backflip turns out to be something you can't do. What then?"

"Then I lose the bet and I'll just have to figure out another way to reach him. This is the opportunity that presented itself and I got to see it through."

"I'm just glad Isaac didn't dunk that ball," I chimed in. "Ain't no way Joe would ever do that." I never learned to be quiet during conversations that didn't involve me.

Joe gave me the side-eye, then he wrapped Yvette in his arms. "Don't worry 'bout me, baby. I got this thing figured out."

She pushed off. "You're all sweaty! Besides, I'm not worried 'bout you. Felicia's graduating soon, so if you go out there and land on your head, then I'm gonna leave you right where you are. I won't have you embarrassing Felicia, showing up at her big night in a brace like some crippled ol' coot!"

"Relax. I ain't gonna embarrass nobody. Ain't nobody knows about this but us and Isaac and his friends and they've probably already forgotten about it anyways."

Joe may have been right about that, but he forgot one important thing that I just mentioned. I don't know how to shut up.

Chapter 16

I never meant to be a gossip hound. In fact, I can say with certainty that I never told important stuff to anyone who didn't need to know, but fun facts are a different story. And Joe's showdown with Isaac fell squarely under the 'Fun Fact' category if you ask me. Plus, I already established that I hate awkward silence.

Checking the mailbox the next day brought such a moment. I saw a neighbor walking by on the other side of the street. The empty air between us liked to have killed me.

"You heard 'bout what Joe's doing?" She confirmed with a head shake that she had not. "Got himself in a dust-up with that good-for-nothing Isaac. He challenged that boy to a backflip contest."

Well, she nearly fell over. "Backflip contest? Joe's way too old for that!"

"That's what I've been telling him, but he's in the backyard training for it right now. Built himself a back-flipping contraption and everything."

Not long after that, I saw a local cat named Jerry at the grocery store. We were both waiting in the check-out line and those things can be pits of despair if you hate awkward silence. Jerry was as flabbergasted as the woman at my mailbox.

"Man, he's a fool! No fifty-year-old got any business tryin' a backflip!"

"I know that's right," I said.

"And with that punk Isaac? Shoot, man, that boy is rotten to the core."

And don't get me started on the center aisle of a church. I was an usher every Sunday evening. Walking ladies to their seats was a surefire, guaranteed high-pressure situation when it came to conversation. An usher is practically mandated to fill the time between the back of the church and the pew with some kind of talk.

"A man his age can't contort himself like that," one lady said, the brim of her colorful hat brushing against my shoulder as she shook her head.

"He must be gone crazy, is all I can figure," I said with a shake of my head, too.

After services, I was standing in the reception line with Pastor Simmons. A long line of people was forming behind me, but I figured the Pastor needed to know why one of his best parishioners was absent from evening services.

"Yes sir, Pastor. That's what happened. He's home training for it as we speak. He never done one before, so it might be best if you kept him in your prayers."

"What'd make him do a thing like that?" The Pastor was beside himself.

"The devil to be sure. Joe got in some sort of challenge with that Isaac boy. You know him, right?"

"Oooh, that's a troubled boy there. Troubled boy."

"Sure as Adam ate the apple, he is!"

"I wish Joe'd think this one through."

"You preaching to the choir now, Pastor." I'm sure he appreciated me relating everything back to church terms.

By Tuesday afternoon, I was locked out of Joe's. He said he couldn't concentrate with me carrying on, so I was banished, just like that. I couldn't quite see into his backyard from mine, so I took my newspaper to a bench at the playground.

Those curly-headed, ten-year-old twins from down the road were sitting beside me. They made an afternoon habit of getting ice cream from the truck that rolled through on the other side of the tracks and they'd eat at the playground. I hadn't really gotten to read the paper yet. I'd caught up on most of the sports news at work, so I was sitting there, fanning myself with it and craning my neck to see over Joe's fence. Those boys were too involved in gobbling that ice cream to talk. Well, it was flat out awkward.

"But Joe was convinced he could beat him at just 'bout anything and that's when that miscreant popped out a great big ol' backflip. Now Joe's gotta do one 'cuz that was the deal." I guess they'd already heard because they couldn't have cared less. "Me and him could be learning to play chess and he's wasting time on this foolish pursuit."

That didn't impress them either.

I sauntered from the bench toward his fence, all stealthy-like. I peeked through a bougainvillea bush right at the instant Joe fell face down and hit the ground hard. It wasn't the first time, judging from the grass stains on the knees of his jeans. He pushed up, brushed off the dirt and untangled himself from the network of pulleys and belts. He let loose with a string of quiet curse words.

Felicia was about seventeen then, and she was sitting on the back steps, watching. Joe didn't know she was there.

"Hey, potty-mouth," she said. "Isn't that what you're trying to get Isaac to stop doing?"

Joe straightened himself up really quick. "Hey baby. How long have you been there?"

"Long enough to see you fall four times in a row."

"Boy, don't I know it? I'm not getting much better. Maybe I should call it off."

"Keep trying, Daddy. You'll get it."

Joe smiled at her. "Maybe your momma is right. Maybe it's something I can't do. I'm missing 'em even with the help of these pulleys. Who knows how bad it'll be without 'em?"

"Don't worry, I covered for you," Felicia said.

"Say what now?"

"I covered for you. I said a prayer just now and will every night for the next two and a half weeks."

"Prayers can't hurt, but I doubt they'll help much at this point."

"I don't doubt it and that's the difference."

Joe unbuckled himself from his contraption and walked over to her. "How so?"

"Remember the scripture you used to read to me when I was little? The one that says if you pray without doubting, mountains can be moved and cast into the sea?"

Joe nodded. "Sure, I remember."

"It was a red-letter passage. That means Jesus said it. Once He gets involved, it ain't up to you anymore."

Joe chuckled. "Guess you really want me to beat that kid, huh?"

"Isaac? I don't care none 'bout Isaac. He won't never amount to nothing. I just think it'd be cool if you did that backflip when everybody says you can't."

"Everybody? Who's been talking?" Right then, Felicia looked straight at the bush I was standing behind. Joe did, too. "Is that so?" he said, looking right at me.

Dang it all, I guess I was about as good at sneaking as I was at whispering.

Chapter 17

It was two weeks later before I finally saw Joe again outside of work. I was hunched down on the sidewalk in front of his house and feeding a hotdog to a mutt. It wasn't Daizy Mae, of course, but just some other stray that had found its way to our neighborhood. I called her predecessor Mojo because he was a boy-dog.

He was whining for the last chunk, and I was doing what I evidently do best.

"Ain't no joke. Joe got up in that boy's face and said, 'Listen here, Isaac, I can do anything you can, you dig?' And that's when that boy did that backflip. Now Joe gotta do one too, or we can't smoke our fish no more. You believe that?"

"Will you give him that hotdog and leave him be?" Joe sniped from his porch. I looked up at him, probably a little too eager.

"Well, if it ain't Mr. Anti-Social," I griped back. "What brings you out to the world of the living this afternoon?"

Joe was stepping gingerly, with a slight limp. He had big sweat rings on his shirt and he was sipping a glass of tea. There was a second glass on the little table between the rockers.

I tossed Mojo the last piece of meat and walked up to the porch. Mojo followed.

"I heard there was a crazy man out here aggravating some poor mongrel," Joe said.

I plopped in the rocker and grabbed the tea. The dog curled up at my feet. "He thinks you're the crazy one, don't ya, boy?"

Mojo liked when I rubbed his belly with my foot. "How's it going back there with the death trap?"

Joe sat next to me. "My legs are stronger than I thought. Must be all those years climbing them ladders."

"How strong they got to be? Little shrimp like you only gotta go up six or seven inches to turn all the way over."

Joe laughed and waved me off.

"You done a real flip yet?" I asked.

"I'm working my way up to it."

"Working your way up to it? Man, you only got a few days!"

"I know," Joe sighed. "That kid probably won't even remember."

"No, he does. I saw his friends the other day and they was saying..." I trailed off.

Joe chuckled. "You're commiserating with the enemy, eh?"

I changed the subject real quick. "You up for a cigar and a drink tonight?"

"Naw. What if Isaac happens by? I can't be smoking if that's what I'm trying to get him to stop doing."

"Aww, come on. You gonna give up everything you love for that thug?"

"I'm in training."

"Just 'cuz you in training don't mean I gotta be too, does it?"

"Smoke and drink yourself silly if you want. I'm not stopping you."

"But you got all the good cigars."

Joe motioned toward his door. "Help yourself."

"And your whiskey's always better than what I got."

"You know where that is, too."

I shuffled my feet, probably a bit too close to a way a toddler stomps around in a tantrum. Mojo got to his feet and wandered off the porch. "Naw, man, it ain't the same. I ain't got no rocker at my place. I'm sitting on the steps every night watching cars go by. Gotta talk to mangy 'ol dogs to pass the time, and he only sticks around 'cuz I'm feeding him tube steaks."

"What about Ed?"

"Ed? He just sits there all quiet watching the game. Every time I talk, he shushes me. He had some kind of fried fish the other night, but it was greasy. He said it was catfish, but it tasted like mud fish. Mud fish ain't no good to eat! Believe me, I know the difference between good eating fish and bad eating fish. Seemed like mud fish is all I'm saying."

Yvette walked out with an ice pack about then. "I hope you're happy, Joe! I told you you'd hurt something. I ain't sticking 'round just so I can watch you kill yourself. I'll load up and go to momma's house." She dropped the pack in Joe's hands.

"Tell the ol' girl I said 'hello'." Joe put the ice pack on his knee and rolled his head from side to side.

"That nerve thing in your neck giving you trouble?" I asked.

"Of course, it is! How could it not be?" Yvette answered for him. "It's his own fool fault, though. Honestly, I don't know how his head ain't popped clean off yet." With that, she went back inside. The door slammed behind her.

"You losing weight?" I asked after I gave Joe a quick once over.

He patted his belly. "I lost a few pounds. 'Bout eight or nine. This training really hits them stomach muscles. I'm starting to see lines in there."

"Maybe, when this is over, we'll call you Joe Six-pack."

"Why does every dude with a six-pack gotta be named 'Joe'?"

Yvette came back out, still ranting. She had a tube of ointment in her hand. "Even Pastor Simmons is keeping next week open in case he got to do your funeral! I told him I won't go to no funeral for a boneheaded stooge. I'll send flowers maybe, but I ain't going." Yvette squirted some ointment in her palm and stood behind Joe. She started to rub his neck over the back of the rocker. "And how am I gonna pay for Felicia's college if you're dead? You ever stop and think of that? Ain't no good can come from this! No good at all!" Joe winced as she used her anger to really get deep into his neck muscles. "Sacrificing so much for a churlish kid like Isaac! Beats all I ever did see. Unmannerly and mean as a snake, is what he is! Trifling! Foolhearty and trifling!"

Out on the sidewalk, a young girl named Kimmy walked by. She was probably eight or nine. "Hi, Mister Moore," she called. "Isaac wants to know if you're gonna back out. He said he'd understand if you did."

That sent Yvette into another tirade. "Back out? Girl, you tell that chump my man's gonna take the cocky wind right of his arrogant sails!"

Joe patted her hand on his right shoulder. "Hey, hey, easy with the smack-talk, baby."

"Don't you 'easy' me! That boy's gotta lotta nerve sending Kimmy over here to spy on you!" She looked back out at Kimmy. "Why you up here doing Isaac's dirty work? He wants to say something, you tell him to come say it his own self!"

"He said he figured he'd give you a chance to call things off so you don't embarrass yourself in front of everybody?"

Joe looked at me again. "Yeah, I know about everybody."

"He said he didn't say nothing to nobody, so he figured you had."

Joe just nodded. "Well, I like that. Shows good character on his part." Another side-eye at me.

"You should get on home before it gets dark now," I added just to hurry that conversation on away from where it seemed to be headed.

"Tell Isaac I'll see him on Friday," Joe said. "Don't worry, Mister Moore. I won't tell him 'bout your knee. He'd just think it's

funny. I hope you beat him, though. I'll be rooting for you."
Kimmy started off with a skip and a wave over her shoulder.

"Then I'll try extra hard," Joe called after her.

Yvette resumed rubbing his neck. "This whole thing gonna give me an ulcer."

Chapter 18

T he fateful Friday came. We worked all day and Joe never said a word. I forgot all about it until we drove home. It was Joe's turn to drive and when he pulled his truck over the tracks, we saw a crowd of no less than thirty people waiting in his front yard.

Isaac was front and center with several of his friends. Yvette was staring him down from the porch with a couple of the neighborhood women by her side. Joe parked and we got out. There were storm clouds forming in the distance. Joe eyed them for a second, but Isaac didn't let him linger on it too long.

"So how 'bout it, Fish Man? You ready to do this?" Isaac had those imaginary muscles in his back flared out again.

Joe broke his stare from the clouds and looked at the crowd with amazement. "Has it been three weeks already?" He went up to his porch, put down his lunch box, and gave Yvette a kiss, like Isaac and the onlookers were afterthoughts. "Hey, baby. How's my lady tonight?"

She turned her head, clearly irritated.

"Three weeks for a backflip. You saying you need more time?" Isaac cawed.

"Nope. A deal's a deal." Joe stayed on the porch and slipped off his work boots and socks. He was walking back down into the yard, barefoot, when Felicia came out and stood by her mother.

Yvette shook her head. "Joe, please..."

Joe held up his hand to Yvette.

I was nearby so I gave my two cents. "Joe, really. This ain't necessary. You ain't got to prove nothing to that kid."

Felicia, though. Felicia wasn't having any of that negative talk. "Do it, Daddy!"

Joe looked right at her and smiled.

I guess I was expecting more build-up, but Felicia had the final say. He winked at her, jumped straight up and did the prettiest backflip I ever did see. He landed perfectly on his feet too, without the slightest stutter step.

It was so sudden, the crowd around him gasped.

Isaac was shocked more than any of us. It only took a moment for him to shake his head and start protesting. "Naw, man, that don't count! I wasn't watching, so--"

Joe must have anticipated this because he leapt up again and did another picture-perfect flip. Everyone lost their collective minds and cheered like I'd never seen. Yvette was dumbfounded along with her friends. I was standing there with my mouth so open I was scared I'd catch a horsefly.

But Felicia? She just rushed down the steps and hugged her daddy tight.

The neighbors erupted again. I finally jumped and cheered. Yvette ran out to join in with Felicia and Joe's embrace. Everyone, including Isaac's friends, gathered around Joe. There was a lot of back-slapping and shouting.

Joe was smiling and shaking hands with everyone until thunder rolled in the distance. Joe looked that way sharply, then bolted for the porch. From the top step, he saw Isaac walking away. By then, he was in front of what would eventually become Felicia's house. Joe ignored the next round of thunder and called out to him.

"Hey! Where do you think you're going?" he barked sternly. Isaac looked back at Joe as everyone else fell silent again. "You owe me something, son!"

"Congratulations," Isaac squeaked.

Joe was on him quick. "I don't want your congratulations. Get over here and throw down those cigarettes you got in your pocket."

Isaac walked slowly. No, he strutted slowly back to Joe's front yard. He had been shown up and his little boy ego was telling him how to appear as though he wasn't humiliated. He stared at Joe as he dropped a pack of cigarettes on the lawn.

"Don't you litter my yard, boy! Bring 'em up and give 'em to me!" A mask of fury was plastered on Joe's face and his eyes ignited with fire. Isaac didn't miss it. He picked the cigarettes up and walked them to the porch. Joe snatched them from him. "Are you done with these for good?" Joe asked, shaking the pack at Isaac.

"That was the deal, wasn't it?" replied Isaac, still trying to look tough.

"How 'bout that filthy talk of yours? You're done with that, too?"

"I said I'd stop, didn't I?"

Joe looked out over the crowd by his porch. "If anybody hears this boy cursing, I wanna know 'bout it, ya hear?"

Isaac postured. "Whatever, man." He started away again.

"Isaac," Joe growled.

"What, man? What?"

"I ain't your man. And don't 'what' me. Try again with some manners and respect."

Isaac slumped his shoulders. Now, I'm not a cowboy so I've never seen a wild bronco get broken. Until, I think, right then.

"Yes... sir?" The words were unfamiliar in his mouth.

"I'm going fishing in the morning. Six-thirty sharp. You be out here." He pointed at the porch stairs. "Right there on that step, ya hear?"

"Fishing? That wasn't no part of the deal." It was as close to a whine as Isaac had ever allowed himself.

"We're done with the deal, son. You be here at six-thirty or I'm gonna come to your house and drag you outta bed, got me?"

Isaac looked at his friends. They'd switched sides a long time ago, so they offered him nothing.

"Yeah."

"What?" Joe was dug in deep and not letting go.

"Yes, sir."

Joe still had that look. "Go on home now."

With that, Isaac walked away. It's a good thing, too. As people in the crowd moved toward Joe to congratulate him again, a bolt of lightning lit the sky and a clap of thunder shook his whole porch. Joe ducked and darted inside the house as everyone else kept cheering. They didn't seem to notice the look of panic on his face, but I did.

Yvette sighed when she whispered to me that he was off to the closet and she hoped he didn't crease her good leather shoes.

Chapter 19

Joe and I had made plans to go fishing that next morning. That was before the whole thing with Isaac. Joe never said I wasn't invited anymore, mainly because I didn't see him the rest of that night. The storm had lasted until well after dark and was followed by another that rolled through a little after ten.

Six-thirty was our usual meeting time, so I stepped out of my front door about then to see if Isaac showed up. If he was there, I figured it was best to let them go it alone. If not, I'd go to Joe's and we'd carry on like it was a normal Saturday.

I sipped my coffee as I looked up past the house between us (again, it didn't yet belong to Felicia) and I was amazed by what I saw. Isaac was sitting on the steps of the porch, right where Joe had told him to be. He was twirling a ball cap, waiting.

I started that way. I was going to mention that if Joe didn't know he was there yet, he might need to knock on the door. I was in front of Joe's when Joe stepped out. Isaac turned and looked up at him.

Way up at him. As if he was on a mountain.

Joe waved him inside and he got up and went. I turned around and loped back to the pitiful front steps of my house. I couldn't help but smile. As the sun rose, I looked East toward the tracks and saw Joe's truck going over them. Isaac's arm hung out my window on the passenger's side.

I suddenly realized why Joe had done what he did, but the full extent wasn't completely clear yet. If the backflips of the previous day happened in moments, then the next part of their story would take years.

I didn't know that then. All I knew was that it was Saturday and I didn't have a thing in the world to do. Then, lo and behold, like an answer to prayer, I saw Mojo ambling over the tracks, coming my way. He was short and squatty and from a distance he could have easily been confused with a black pig.

I didn't know what I'd do for the rest of the day, but right then I had a duty and that was to go inside and rustle up some hotdogs.

Chapter 20

It took a few weeks, but the duo that Isaac and Joe had become eventually became a trio. I tagged along for the fishing trips at first, then was a part of them, or better yet, Isaac was a part of me and Joe. Thinking back now, those days might as well have blurred into a single afternoon. I can only remember an instance or two of the things we did hundreds of times over days and months that stretched out into years.

We adopted him into our crew and taught him everything we knew. There were times he needed a place to stay. Because Isaac's momma was in and out of jail during that time, and Felicia was still in Joe's house, Isaac stayed with me. Joe taught him how to throw the cast-net. I taught him how to throw a fade away jumper. He learned to drive in Joe's truck. He learned to speed and turn into the skid in mine. Joe took him to church. I took him to the races at the county speedway. Now, I don't mean to say I kept him in touch with the streets while Joe made him a gentleman. We each did a little bit of both. I took him to his science fairs. He had his first beer with Joe.

Anyway, the short story is we both raised him up for those six or seven years the best way we knew how. He liked basketball, so we taught him the real fundamentals of team play, not the pick-up game trash he had learned up until then. He could gut a mullet and prepare the smoker better than Joe or me after a while. He grew strong. And he was polite. He never cursed and he didn't smoke or get into the drug scene, like some of his old friends unfortunately did. He could even bake like a champ because Yvette wasn't going to let no boy come through her house without knowing how to cook.

The thing he did the best, though, was the thing we lacked. That boy was smart. His IQ was off the charts. Felicia helped him with his math and science homework until he took off into the stratosphere beyond her. He picked up Spanish super-easy.

Now, I'm not saying we made him smart. He'd always been that. He already knew the math and language and science stuff. He learned it all in school and absorbed it from society. He finally just allowed himself to admit he knew it. It was like a plant that grows underground for a long time, building its root system. Once it pops up from the soil, it seems to grow faster than all the plants around it. That was Isaac.

Isaac was studying something or other in one of the rockers on Joe's porch. Joe came out with two books. One was a new Bible. The other was a thick volume called 'The Complete Works of William Shakespeare'.

"I suppose between Shakespeare and the Bible, 'bout every story that can be told is."

Isaac took the books and smiled up at Joe, waiting for more advice or words of wisdom. Joe just turned and went back inside. I'll be darned if Isaac didn't read both of those voluminous tomes. Took him a year or so, but he did it. Joe never asked him if he did, but it became clear because stories from both popped up in his regular conversation.

Not that Joe or I could keep up. I don't think Joe knew too much about Shakespeare, although he did buy a second Shakespeare book for himself and tried to get through it after he gave the one to Isaac. I don't think he got too far into it before he gave up. I doubt he ever read the Bible in its entirety either. I know I didn't. We knew all we knew about it from church. Isaac knew both books inside and out because, we found out later, he had a photogenic memory.

He joined the church choir with Yvette. He got into all kinds of clubs at school and was president of the student body or some such. He made the varsity basketball team as a sophomore and was the best player in the county by the time he was a senior. Without going into every little detail, suffice it to say that Isaac made a 180 degree turn after Joe did that backflip. He excelled in everything that he ever tried and that is no exaggeration. To top it off, he graduated as the Valedictorian of his class and gave a beautiful speech at his graduation. He even thanked his 'Two Dads' and looked at me and Joe. Everybody in the audience looked at us and kind of giggled. I don't know why. It was true. We were like his two dads. I thought we deserved a round of applause, so I gave me and Joe a standing ovation right there by myself.

To prove I'm not full of it, I could point to a drawer crammed with college acceptance letters that came to my address for Isaac. He looked at and considered them all, but late in his Senior year, he narrowed it down to two.

West Point and the University of Florida. He wanted to meet with Joe about his decision, so we sat at the little table in the nook by my kitchen. He desperately wanted Joe's opinion and guidance on the biggest decision of his life.

Joe looked over both letters. "That's a nice basketball scholarship to State. But an appointment to West Point? Son, that's hard to pass up."

"I'm thinking UF. They've been to the Final Four twice in the last three years and I can get a business degree for my post-NBA enterprises. Not many people make the NBA from West Point." Isaac seemed to have his mind made up. He was just seeking Joe's approval.

I haven't mentioned as of yet how that was a hard thing to come by for Isaac. Joe held back praise for him. That was my role, I guess. Joe took on a stern disposition around him. I found it to be uncharacteristic of him and completely opposite of how he dealt with Felicia. I can't say I totally agreed with Joe's treatment of Isaac at times.

I clapped. "Hot diggity dog! You're going to be a Gator! How 'bout that? Full ride until you're eligible for the National Basketball Association! My boy, look at you!"

We high-fived across the table, but Joe just leaned back heavily in his chair. Then, he shook his head. "I just think about all that science you love so much. All that science and you gonna do what? Sell cars? Don't that just beat all?"

"Ain't nobody said nothing about selling cars," I chided. "Where do you get that from?"

"What else he gonna do with an economics degree? Cars. Stocks. He gonna sell something to somebody. That's what it's for."

"No, the degree is for after my pro career. You know, my second job after I retire. Haven't you been listening? I'm going to play basketball in the pros. Their program is built for that. It feeds players to the NBA on the regular."

Isaac was fiery. He was pure and smart and all the good things that he turned out to be, but he was also extremely passionate about stuff he believed in. Sometimes his passion exposed itself in what could be mistaken for aggressiveness. Especially with Joe.

"Oh, yeah, I've been listening. You gonna make it big in college, then you gonna make it big in the pros. I heard you. But let me tell ya, all those people polluting your head trying to convince you to gamble your whole future on a pipe dream ain't gonna be around when it don't happen."

"How is going to UF on a full ride for basketball gambling my future?" Isaac stood up so fast when he said that the chair shot back into the wall behind him. "This is a chance of a lifetime!"

Joe was calm and measured. "That scholarship is for half basketball and half academics."

"So? It's all paid for!" Isaac barked.

"The basketball half is to make you put the team first. The academic half is in case they want to cut your basketball portion. If they were sure you would be of great value to the team, then the program would give it all to you."

Isaac turned completely around and flung his arms. "That makes no sense! You're not making sense!"

"Then I'll tell ya what I know as plainly as I can, Isaac. The professional basketball career is not happening for you. Not in a million years. Don't get this all backwards. You used basketball for as long as you needed it and it was a lot of fun. It got you where you are now. But you got to use that brain from here on out. Go to West Point. They make winners for life there."

"And forget basketball? I'm one of the best in the country. Those papers say so. You want me to just throw it all away?"

"They have two good point guards ahead of you. One is a junior and one is a red-shirt freshman. Those two might make the pros. If you're lucky, they'll graduate ahead of you and you might start one year. And that's only if they don't get other blue chip players next year that they'll put ahead of you. You're their insurance policy for the two on the roster now. They get someone next year or the year after and you'll stay on the bench with several years invested in an economics program. You'll be behind on the things you're destined to do." Isaac slammed the table with his fists. It made me jump, but Joe didn't bat an eye. "You came here, showed me your options, and asked for my advice. I'm not gonna hold a gun to your head to make you follow it. You're a man now. You gotta do what's best for yourself."

Isaac snatched up his papers and stormed from my house. "You're never happy! You're not as good as me at anything, but I still can't make you happy! In three years, I could be making millions! You can't say that! There was never a time in your life when you could!" Isaac slammed the door behind him so hard it rattled some pictures in my hallway.

I glared at Joe, but he just looked down and frowned.

The next day, Isaac signed his letter of intent at a ceremony with his high school principal and his guidance counselor standing nearby. A recruiter with the Army was there and hopeful he'd get Isaac's commitment. The Basketball Coach at UF didn't show. He sent an assistant coach in his stead. I was there with Yvette and Isaac's momma. Joe wasn't invited.

Isaac put on the Gator hat and signed their letter to thunderous applause.

Chapter 21

Over the next two years, Joe and Isaac made amends. Isaac sent us Gator ball caps every few months, so we always had new ones. Since the campus was only a couple hours away, we drove to a game or two. Unfortunately, Isaac never played when we were there. He did get some minutes on the court, just never in meaningful games. It was a thrill to see him the handful of times he came on during televised games, though.

The Gators got a few more A-list players to play his position in the subsequent years and Isaac fell down the depth chart. An unfortunate twist to his knee finished the downward process that was already well underway. Isaac didn't play his third year. Instead, he threw himself into his studies. He had changed his major after his first year and, of course, he did well in his new path. He graduated in three years with a double major in some science or another and a minor in something else. Stuff I'm not sure I could even pronounce. Not Economics. That's all I knew.

His momma did another stint in prison during his UF years, so he stayed with me on breaks. Joe would take us fishing and we didn't talk about Isaac's future. He was doing fine without our input. We went to his college graduation since his momma was still in the clink, and he let us in on some big news when we took him out to dinner afterwards.

"I already have a position at the high school," Isaac said. "I can teach science or math and help coach the basketball team. They'll let me step right in and start this August."

Yvette clapped over her clam strips. "Oh, Isaac! Felicia loves her second graders. And high school could be just the beginning. You could move up to college level after a few years, then go into administration, smart as you are."

"College president," I echoed. "Boy, that's outta sight."

"Well, teaching is certainly a noble profession," Joe said. "I saw a house for sale down the road from us. It's a nice house. Probably could pick it up cheap and fix it up how you wanted." Isaac grinned at Joe's approval. "Welcome back to the neighborhood, son. Don't bother with a mower right away. You can use mine." Joe turned a little insolent then. Isaac must have caught it because his smile faded. "I mow on Saturday, so you'll have to mow on Sunday. But we can sit on my porch and sip iced tea when you're done. Yvette makes the best. It's good on a hot day."

I didn't realize what was happening and neither did Yvette, I don't think, but Joe and Isaac were at it again.

"What's that supposed to mean?" Isaac said.

"Well, he's right. Yvette makes the best tea this side of--" I started but Isaac interrupted me.

"No, he's saying I'm a failure if I go that route! He's saying I'll be just like you two and that's bad."

Yvette looked crossly at Joe. "Is that what you're saying, Joe? What's so wrong with our life? What's wrong with being a teacher? Your own daughter is a teacher."

"He don't mean that," I piped in. "We would love to have you back in town, Isaac. You can stay at my place for as long as you need. And I got my own mower. We don't need his."

Joe just stared hard at Isaac. "You're perceptive, I'll give you that."

"I've never had a penny to my name. What's so terrible about me getting a job and making good money and working my way up from there?" Isaac said it loud enough that other diners looked our way.

"There's forty or more teachers down at the high school," Joe gruffed. "Good people making huge impacts on kids every day. There's also forty or so at the high school the next town over. They'd love you to join their ranks. Heck, they'd be lucky if you did."

Yvette patted Isaac's arm. "Don't listen to him, Isaac. It's getting close to his bedtime and he's getting cranky." She shot a death glare at Joe meant to back him off.

"Just drop the sarcasm and say whatever is on your mind, Mister Moore," Isaac said.

"Okay," Joe obliged. "This can't be your only opportunity. What else do you have?"

Isaac shrugged. "I also applied for a Physician's Assistant Program. It's a two-year course, and I have a friend whose dad is a cardiologist. He said he'd pay my way if I worked for him when I got out."

I applauded that. "No loans to pay back! That's a good deal!"

"Physician Assistant's school? Gonna work for a cardiologist and give medicine to a bunch of old, fat people like me who can't keep hamburgers and moon pies outta their faces. Son, if you wanna push pills on a bunch of people who won't help themselves, you coulda sold the same drugs your daddy did."

Isaac pushed away from the table. Yvette was irate when she whispered hoarsely at Joe. "What is wrong with you? For crying out loud, I don't know how you can be so negative on such a happy night." She gathered up her purse and stood up. "Come on, Isaac. Let's me and you go get some ice cream. I saw a place on the way here."

"He ain't telling us something, Yvette." Joe didn't budge from his seat. "You have another option. You told your momma and she told me. Why won't you consider it?"

"I applied on a lark," Isaac said. "The tuition at Cornell is insane. The loans would cripple me for years. I'm just ready to be done with school and get on with my life."

Joe moved his plate to the side and folded his hands in front of him. "You can be one of forty teachers in one school, or you can be one Physician's assistant out of a few thousand in the country or you can be something else."

Isaac stared back at him. Joe wasn't done. "You're one in a million, Isaac. One in a billion maybe. Better than me or Yvette or him." He pointed at me nonchalantly with his thumb. "Better than my own daughter or anyone else in this restaurant or at the University of Florida. You're better than anyone you'll meet at Cornell, too, but you gotta go there to see that. I'm begging you, Isaac, don't settle for a life that's beneath you. You need me to cosign for your loans, I'll do it. Put my house up as collateral. Whatever you need, I'll be there." He motioned to me and Yvette. "We'll be there. But you gotta go all in and trust yourself. As a teacher, you'll help hundreds. As a physician's assistant, you'll help hundreds, too. God put you here to help millions. I truly believe that."

Isaac grabbed Yvette by the arm. "Pick Missus Moore up at the Mon Delice Bakery and Ice Cream Shop in about an hour." The two turned and walked out of the restaurant, arm in arm, but noticeably dejected.

We waited around a while for the check, but neither of us spoke. Finally, I said, "I used to wonder why you bothered with him. Now I wonder why he bothers with you. Why are you so hard on him? Why can't you give him no props? The boy's doing great. Least you can do is say so from time to time."

"He don't need no props from me," Joe glowered. "He can get that from anyone. Shoot, everyone else is just glad to see him become anything but a junky or a dealer. Who's gonna be the one who keeps driving him so he can get what he really wants?"

"You, I reckon," I said. "But how do you know what he really wants?"

"Because he keeps asking. I don't have any idea what he really wants, but he does. It just seems too far out of reach for him right now. He needs someone to keep him marching down that road because he can hear his daddy's footsteps right behind him and they're gaining."

"I'm just saying you should share a little joy with him, that's all."

"When he gets where he needs to be, he'll know it. And he won't need any more approvals or props. Not from me or anyone else. He'll know it and he won't ask."

We sat in silence until the bill was paid. On our way out to his truck, I asked Joe, "Where's Cornell anyway?"

"Ithaca, New York."

"That's a long way away, Joe. Why are you trying to get him to go so far?"

"Because it's an Ivy League school."

I perked up then. "Ivy League? That's great news, but I thought he was done with ball."

Joe just shook his head. "Man, you're so hard to take sometimes."

Isaac didn't come home for the summer after that night. He didn't take the job at the high school or go to Physician's Assistant school. He went right up to that school in New York and got started. We didn't see him much after that.

To my dismay, we didn't see him much at all for a long time.

Chapter 22

The years rolled on like they tend to do. Joe and Yvette's hallway was flooded with framed pictures that were a testament to that.

There was one of Joe and Yvette with a cruise ship in the background. After years of no vacations, they started taking annual cruises and loved them. There was a picture of the two by a Christmas tree. Joe had given Yvette some diamond earrings that year. She was near tears.

Another showed me and Joe eating cake at our retirement party, looking at the camera with big, proud smiles. It was in a bigger warehouse than the one where I arm-wrestled Jackie, but the vibe was the same. I could have retired a year or two before Joe, but I waited on him so we could have a party together. What else did I have to do?

In another picture, Joe had his ear on one side of Felicia's pregnant belly and Yvette was on the other. They both made goofy faces.

Wonderful times, they were. Felicia had that baby boy and bought the house right smack between Joe and me. Everything was perfect, except that Isaac was gone from us. It had been almost ten years since his college graduation.

Until, one night, not long after Joe's 68th birthday.

Joe and I were sitting on his porch, rocking in our chairs. We weren't drinking or smoking cigars that night. We were just sitting, watching the sun go down.

When a black BMW rolled over the tracks and started up Doreen Street, I couldn't help but whistle.

"Nice ride," I said in awe. It was sleek and classy. Not at all gaudy like Manny's car.

Joe just nodded. It slowed in front of Joe's house and, much to my surprise, pulled into the driveway. The car parked and the door opened and out stepped a big, tall, strong, knock-you-dead-handsome man.

Isaac.

Doctor Isaac Dawkins.

Our boy.

I was so excited I almost tripped over myself getting down the steps to see him. We hugged and laughed and all that, but when I looked to see where Joe was, I saw that he was still on the porch, just sitting.

"You steal that car?" Joe asked as Isaac and I walked toward the porch, arm and arm.

"No sir, Mister Moore. Bought it fair and square," Isaac chuckled.

"Well, you've been gone a long time. I figured you got thrown in jail or something."

Here we go, I thought. *Joe just can't let a good thing be.*

Isaac unwrapped his arm from mine and walked to the first step up to the porch, but he stopped right there. He looked up at Joe.

"I'm a surgeon, but you already knew that. You're always snooping around behind me, checking into my business."

Joe just rocked a couple of times in his chair. "I can't help it if your momma wants to brag on you every time that I call her. What'd you go moving her to that condo way out on the beach for? Made my phone bills go way up. I ought to start calling her collect if all she's gonna do is blabber on 'bout you."

Isaac just smiled. Actually, Joe wouldn't let me call him Isaac anymore, even though Isaac insisted on it. To Joe, and me by extension, it was Dr. Dawkins from there on out. He'd earned the title, Joe said. We owed it to him to call him that. So, he did and I did, too.

"What's your specialty again?"

"Neonatal neurosurgery," Dr. Dawkins said in his kind, humble way.

Joe looked at me. "Don't that beat all? Our boy here is a neurosurgeon for neonates."

"Neo-whats?" I gasped. "You told me he was a people doctor!" I was kidding then. I knew what neonates were.

Dr. Dawkins laughed, but Joe snorted irritably. "Jeez, bubba," he whispered. I looked at Dr. Dawkins and winked. I could get under Joe's skin when I wanted to, that's for sure.

I went up the steps and waved for Dr. Dawkins to follow. Figured it was a good time for him and Joe to hug, but Dr. Dawkins didn't move. He stood quiet for a moment, still looking up at Joe. Way up, like Joe was on a mountain.

Dr. Dawkins said, "How'd you know?"

"Know what?" Joe replied.

"That I could be anything more than my father? I was nothing but trouble and you poured everything you had into me. You did that backflip right over there." He pointed out into the yard.

"Two of them, by golly. I can still do 'em too, so don't go getting no ideas."

Dr. Dawkins laughed. "I don't doubt it. All those fishing trips. All that time you spent helping me with homework and picking me up for church and buying me books."

Joe looked at me. "Shakespeare and the Bible. All the stories that can be told are right there."

"I talk to people about you," Dr. Dawkins continued. "I tell them what you did for me. No one could believe you extended yourself like that when we weren't even kin."

"Now that's a relative term, ain't it?"

"You know how dangerous it was for you to try backflips back then?"

"I did them because I wanted you to see me do something that should have been impossible. Then you'd know you could do the impossible, too. And growing up out of the pit you were in had to seem that way."

"It wouldn't have cost you a thing if I turned out like I should have."

"You did turn out like you should have, son. I had an ache in my brain 'bout you. Sort of like an itch that wouldn't let me rest until I made a stand for you. That's all it was really. I didn't have a choice. The itch was that bad."

"Sounds to me like a worm. They make medicine for brain worms, Doc?" I asked. Sometimes, when I really tried to be funny, I absolutely wasn't.

Joe just shrugged and looked at me. "Actually, it was a lot like a worm. I thought about that feeling for a long time." He looked back at Dr. Dawkins. "Figured it must be the finger of God. He does that sometimes, ya hear? Goes sticking His finger deep in your mind and scratches around 'til you can't help but do something. You felt it too, Isaac, but it was about yourself. You knew you were special. You just needed someone to keep you from making excuses. It'd have been a shame if you limited yourself without knowing any better."

"He did ride you hard," I said looking at the good doctor. "But Lord, you was an ornery little so and so. Sometimes I wondered why you two stuck it out with each other."

"But we did." Joe smiled that million-dollar smile at Dr. Dawkins. "And look at you now. You're saving babies. There ain't no bigger calling in the world than that."

Dr. Dawkins came up the steps then and looked Joe in the eye. He finally wrapped his long, strong arms around his frail little mentor.

And I think Joe cried a little.

We had dinner that night. All of us, together again. Dr. Dawkins, Yvette, Felicia, Willie, Joe, and I had the time of our lives. We talked and laughed for hours.

We were a family. And family is the mightiest force in nature.

Chapter 23

Six months after that glorious night, Willie took sick. We watched him dwindle before our eyes. Felicia exhausted all possibilities in his treatment. Dr. Dawkins did, too.

There was just nothing else that could be done. They were forced to accept it when Felicia and Yvette met Dr. Dawkins and his colleague, a world-renowned pediatric neurosurgeon, in Dr. Dawkins's office.

It was also the day the jagged white man showed up on Doreen Street.

Yvette and Felicia weren't home yet from their visit with Dr. Dawkins. We were still meandering around between Joe's yard and the playground, worrying over Willie. I'd called 911 thirty minutes before a police cruiser came over the tracks and stopped in front of where Joe was pushing Willie in the swing. It wasn't an official cruiser, but a patrol car used by the Auxiliary Police Force in our community.

Deputy Bill, in his late 70s and still powerfully built, but heavier than years before, stepped out of the car. His forearm tattoo was still visible, though distorted with age and sun damage. He retired from the Sheriff's Department a few years prior and was working part-time as a liaison between the city police department and our neighborhood and other neighborhoods like ours. Bill had certainly earned that position since our night at the tracks so long before. He had spent much of his time genuinely reconciling with our community and he had done very well.

"Howdy doo, fellas," Bill said with a friendly wave. I waved back and Joe pulled Willie from the swing and walked toward him. They shook hands. "Was that you who reported a trespasser?"

"Sure was. White guy. He left a few minutes ago," Joe replied.

"What was he doing?" Bill draped his thick arms across the top of his car door and looked from Joe to me.

"Well, he appeared under that tree and started wandering around and he walked funny," Joe blurted in a single breath while pointing to the oak across the street.

"Appeared?"

Joe nodded. I stood by Joe and took Willie from his arms. "He was drunker than all get out is what I think," I added.

"Where was he trespassing?" Bill asked.

Joe pointed out some homes well down the road. "Ida Macon's house and the Haynes's. They aren't home, but Jamal and Evelyn Sheldon saw him and talked to him when he went into their yard. And Manny, too. You know Manny?"

"Oh yeah. We know Manny quite well down at the department." He shielded his eyes from the sun and looked where Joe pointed. "That's quite a piece down there. How'd you see him?"

Joe didn't answer, as if ashamed.

"We trained some binocs on him," I said. Figured he needed to hear the truth regardless of how paranoid it sounded.

"You talk to him?"

"He didn't really talk. He just made funny noises and whistled a lot," I went on.

"He come up on Felicia's house, then he tried to grab Willie," Joe added. Bill perked up at that.

"Whoa, now! Like kidnap him?" He dropped his arms from the top of the door and let them hang by his side, as if he was keeping them close to his holster in case he needed his pistol. It was reflex, I assume, because he didn't carry a firearm anymore. At least not a department issued one.

Joe slumped as if he was suddenly sorry for having Bill come out. "He tried to, uh, he tried to touch him on the head. We stopped that before it happened, but he brushed his cheek with his finger."

Bill nodded. "Uh huh. Then what?"

"He said 'mine'." It took me by surprise when Joe said that.

"Mine?"

"Yeah," Joe continued. His voice started to quiver. "Like he was saying that Willie belonged to him. Like he was claiming him."

Bill looked at me. "You hear that?"

"He was hissing a lot." I knew I had to back up Joe's story, but I don't think I sold it very well. "Like a snake. You know? Hissing through his teeth. That's what I heard. I mean, it was hard to make out with the hissing, but he definitely said 'mine'." My expression must have betrayed me, because I don't think Bill believed that I heard a thing. Which, of course, I hadn't.

Bill looked back at Joe. "Then what?"

"He went back to the tree and vanished." Joe said it, but I could tell he didn't want to.

Bill turned to me again. I saw the sympathy on his face. "Did you see him vanish?"

"Well, he, um, ya see," I was stuttering and didn't know exactly why. I knew I should be supporting Joe's story to the bitter end, no matter how crazy it sounded. "He disappeared pretty quick. I was running up to get the phone and when I turned around, he was gone." I pointed to the oak.

Bill looked at Joe with concern. Joe backed away, knowing his accusations were thin. "If he didn't take anything, I can't do much about it, Joe. It ain't against the law for a white guy to be here."

"It's got nothing to do with him being white!" Joe snatched Willie from my arms and spun back toward the swings. "Forget it, Bill! Forget we even called!"

"I'm just saying, Joe."

"I know what you're saying! I know!"

Bill's tone was suddenly apologetic. "I'll look around and see if I come across him. If I do, I'll stop him and run his name, okay?"

Joe stomped back to the swings and put Willie in one.

I turned back to Bill, who tipped his hat to me. "It's hot today. Might get him outta the sun, huh?"

I nodded, not knowing what else to do.

Chapter 24

A while after Bill left, we sat on the porch, Joe in his rocker and me in mine. Willie raced his truck around the wooden slats beneath our feet. Joe was downtrodden and didn't speak. He just stared off at the oak.

I saw Felicia's car cross the tracks. She drove by us and parked sideways in her yard, between her house and the power pole, but closer to the house than she was that morning. That was good. Yvette was able to open her door at least.

"They're back," I said to nudge Joe from his stupor. He jolted himself from his daydream and watched as Yvette walked toward us, holding back tears. Felicia sat in the car a moment, but finally got out and slammed the door. The noise drew Willie's attention and he lit up when he saw his mom coming his way.

"Was Willie good for you boys?" Yvette asked, wiping her eyes.

"Yep," Joe said.

"Nothing but a joy," I added. "As always."

"How was the ride?" Joe asked.

"Long," replied Yvette. "I hate that traffic over there."

Felicia stomped up the steps and grabbed Willie under the arms. She lifted him to her hip.

"Daddy, he's filthy!" she snapped. Yvette went inside to hide the fact that she was upset. Felicia dealt with her sorrow by letting her anger flare and she didn't try to hide that one bit.

"Tell me about it," I said with a smile. "My dungarees are still full of sand."

"Did he even get a nap?" she kept on. People just weren't finding me funny that day.

Joe followed Yvette inside. I wasn't far behind because Felicia was boring a hole in the side of my head with a death glare.

In the kitchen, Yvette was busying herself at the counter, pulling out pots and pans and such. Joe stepped up behind her and wrapped his arms around her waist.

"I was 'bout to make the Lima Beans Felicia likes so much. Thought it'd go good with the ribs. Y'all did quit with your shenanigans long enough to smoke ribs, didn't you?"

"What'd they say?" Joe asked in a soothing tone.

"Or I could make some black-eyed peas. It wouldn't take--" Joe spun her around and hugged her. She immediately began sobbing into his shoulder.

After a moment of holding her tight, Joe whispered calmly. "What did they say about Willie?"

"They said there's nothing we can do," she bawled.

"I don't believe that. Doctor Dawkins must be able to do something." He cooed the words, still trying to be calming even though his sentiment was combative.

Yvette saw through it and pushed back from him. "No, Joe, he can't! Nobody can. All we can do is keep Willie happy. We don't let him know what's happening and just keep loving him."

Joe's calm tone was suddenly gone. "And watch him die?"

Yvette broke away completely from his embrace. She leaned heavily on the counter and gasped in deep heaves.

"I'm calling Doctor Dawkins," Joe said as if it were a matter of fact.

"Because we didn't say the right things? Because you thought of something nobody else has?" Yvette's sorrow gave way to that same fury Felicia had put on full display on the porch. It was a family trait, I guess. "You gonna lecture him again over something he can't do nothing about? You're not calling him! You leave that poor man alone for once in your life and stop bullying him!"

"I ain't giving my baby boy up." The first tear formed in the corner of Joe's eye. Yvette's despair had landed firmly on him.

"So, I guess you think I am?" Yvette slapped Joe across the shoulder. "How dare you?" Joe tried to move in for another hug, but Yvette wasn't having it. She pushed him away. "There's no way for you to understand," she stammered. "If I could die…" She had to take big gulping breaths to keep from bawling again. "I swear it, Joe, if I could just…" He worked his way into the embrace again. She didn't resist. "Not even to save him, but to just give him one more day with our little girl," she continued. "This is killing Felicia. I don't know what's worse. Watching what's happening to him or watching what's happening to her."

Joe's eyes gushed forth their tears as he dropped his face in her shoulder. He stroked the back of her head though, comforting her even in his own anguish.

"She's losing her baby and I'm losing mine!" She buried her face in Joe's neck. Joe held her tight and they cried together.

A bit later, Joe sat in his recliner in his living room and dabbed his eyes with his handkerchief. I sat on the couch across from him, taking little sips of tea because my throat hurt so bad from choking back tears that it wasn't easy to swallow.

Down the hall, Yvette was drawing Willie a bath. She sang sweetly to him while she put him in. I could hear him giggling and her laughing with him. He splashed about. He sure loved his bath time.

Felicia entered the living room, went straight to Joe and sat in his lap. Joe hugged her close to him.

"My girl," he soothed.

"Oh Daddy," she groaned in a low whisper.

"He's gonna be alright. He's gonna be just fine. Wait and see."

"No, Daddy. It's hopeless."

"Baby, baby. Ain't nothing ever hopeless."

Felicia shook her head as she lowered it against his shoulder. "Isaac said so."

"It don't matter what he says. Not as long as mountains can be moved and cast into the sea."

She popped her head up and looked at him. Her tears really started then. She curled her legs up on his lap and rested her head on his shoulder again. He started rocking in the recliner.

For once, I knew enough to shut my mouth and not say anything. Joe rocked Felicia as she cried, a little girl just needing her daddy again.

Now, obviously, I wasn't there with Dr. Dawkins when Joe's call came in, but I always imagined he was at his desk looking at a CT scan on a computer monitor or prepping for surgery or something important. He could have been at the gym or on the links for all I know. All I do know for certain was that Joe was gripping his phone like he was strangling a snake when Dr. Dawkins picked up on the other end. Joe was staring out the living room window into the front yard.

I couldn't hear what Dr. Dawkins was saying on his end, but Joe's responses were enough to give me the gist.

"Isaac," Joe gruffed when Dr. Dawkins answered. It shocked me that he would call our good doctor by his first name, especially since he was the one who had forbidden all of us from doing it once Isaac had earned the title.

"Mister Moore," he returned, not wanting to commit the same breach of etiquette that Joe just had.

"I won't accept that nothing can be done about my grandson."

"Mister Moore, believe me when I say that I sympathize with your family, but there is nothing more we can do."

Well, that set Joe right off. "My family? What is that supposed to mean, Isaac? You're going into full impersonal doctor mode on me, just like that?"

"Our family," Dr. Dawkins corrected himself. "You know I consider your family to be mine."

"Then fix him, son. You're a neurosurgeon. This is something you're perfectly capable of doing. Fix Willie so we can move on from this."

"Mister Moore, you have to understand that--"

"That my grandbaby is going to die?"

I think that the combination of Joe calling him by his first name and making unreasonable, oversimplified demands got Dr. Dawkins in a bit of a huff. He fired back with enough vim and vinegar that I could hear his voice through the phone. "It's a horrible, horrible thing, Mister Moore! I can't stand it anymore than you can, and I know it isn't fair, but it can't be prevented or treated! No more than an earthquake or a hurricane can be prevented or stopped! It's an arbitrary, freak accident of nature and an unjustified, an, an unforeseeable..." I think his voluminous vocabulary failed him in the heat of the moment. He paused, then settled on a rote cliche. "It's just an act of God."

Joe was very measured in his response. More than I was expecting. It could have broken down into an argument that used to be so typical between those two, where Joe chest-bumped and Isaac threw up defenses and finally got mad and stormed off. Somehow, though, I think Joe recognized Isaac, I mean Dr. Dawkins, was genuinely hurting, too. He had truly done all he could. He knew he was supposed to do something for Willie, his young 'nephew' by proxy. I think Joe got a sense of guilt from Isaac. Once again, Joe took the weight of the moment on his shoulders.

"An act of God? That's you, Isaac. What God put in your hands, in your mind, those are His acts. Not some failure in my grandson's skull. God's will ain't done by malignant tumors. It's done when you do exactly what it is you've been put here to do. His glory shines in you, just like it shines in Willie's grinning face now, a year from now, ten years from now."

"That's the thing, Mister Moore," Dr. Dawkins said, suddenly calm again. "He doesn't have a year. He may not even have to-morrow."

"I'll get him to tomorrow, Isaac. You get him beyond that."

It was an odd thing for Joe to say. I didn't really know where his thoughts were going, but even Joe wasn't so sharp witted that he didn't get ahead of himself and say goofy, nonsensical things sometimes. Turns out, this wasn't one of those times. It was the most astute thing he said all day.

"The surgery that Willie needs is out of my scope of exper-tise."

"Why? Because you only learned to operate on babies? Come on, now."

"Yes. That's exactly why."

"You can operate. Pediatric patients and neonatal patients can't be all that different."

"They are. Absolutely, they are. Neonates don't get what he has. I just can't do what you're demanding me to do."

"Son, I've never demanded anything of you. I've only ex-pected you to do what you're capable of doing. If you don't know that yet, then you haven't been paying attention to what I've been trying to show you in all of our time together."

"What Willie has is so malicious and hostile that there is no proven surgical intervention for it and all of the attempts at any experimental procedures have failed."

Joe smiled and nodded as if Dr. Dawkins could see him. "So, you've been researching some experimental surgeries?"

"Of course, I have. It's all I've been doing since we diagnosed him. I'm looking at obscure and fringe surgical techniques right now. But they don't work. That's why no one will touch him. Experimental treatments. Accepted procedures. They have the same result because his type of tumor is one hundred percent fatal, one hundred percent of the time."

"Take those experimental surgeries that you have researched, put them with the standard treatments and mix them together. Identify where they fail. Then, do better. You're smarter than all the guys who've tried before you."

"Any approach I would try is completely untested and fully theoretical. There's no dependable blueprint for what his surgery would require. The problems that could arise while going in blind and without the proper tools could be catastrophic," Dr. Dawkins said. "The equipment I would need hasn't even been made yet."

"There we go," Joe piped with excited optimism. "Real medicine! Not retreading what's been done but creating new healing pathways. No robots or computers leading the way. Just man versus nature in its most ruthless form. Embrace the spirit of discovery. Break down the barriers that everyone else has accepted. That's how the world is changed. That's what you were made for, son!"

"I won't do that, Mister Moore. I won't experiment on Willie."

"Why not? You think your hospital won't allow it for malpractice reasons?" Joe assumed. "We don't care. We'll sign away all liability. We won't sue you or the hospital or anybody. Just get him in there and do your thing. Find the way to heal him."

"It's not about malpractice."

"Then what is it?"

It took a moment for Dr. Dawkins to say what he needed to say. I could hear his voice breaking through the phone. "What if he dies in surgery? With you and Felicia and Missus Moore waiting and praying and putting all the faith you have in God on me? How could I come out of there and face you all?"

Every person Joe talked to in that hour had cried on him and needed his assurance. Dr. Dawkins was no different.

"You could come out knowing we'd be thankful he had you by his side with your hand in his. We'd be grateful knowing you were there fighting for him to the very last second. We wouldn't want it any other way."

A long moment passed, and Dr. Dawkins didn't say anything.

"Get him into the hospital tomorrow. Call Felicia and work it out, ya hear?"

"Yes sir." That part I heard.

Joe punched his phone's screen to disconnect. He looked at me.

"You alright?" I asked him.

"Let's take a walk," he said.

And so, we did.

Chapter 25

Joe and I walked on the sidewalk on the other side of the street from our houses. Daizy Mae followed us, her leash dragging along behind her. I kept her on our trail by occasionally flipping a vanilla crème cookie her way. She would slurp it off the hot concrete and keep trotting after us.

Joe and I stopped in front of Jamal and Evelyn's house. They were sitting on their porch, waving away the late afternoon gnats. Jamal hailed us happily when we walked up the driveway.

"What's new, fellas?" he gushed. "Got you a tagalong, huh?" Daizy Mae darted past my legs to the porch and sat at Jamal's feet. Evelyn leaned over and stroked Daizy Mae's head.

"Well, good afternoon, Pismo," she said as Jamal reached down and petted the mongrel, too. Daizy Mae lapped up the affection. I guess ol' Daizy Mae worked a circuit in our neighborhood and had a different name at every spot. For the life of me, I don't know how they figured her to be a 'Pismo'. That name didn't fit at all.

"I call her Daizy Mae," I said, certain that they would hear my name for her and immediately agree it was perfect.

Evelyn chuckled. "That's a cow's name."

"Yeah," Jamal said. "My grandpa had two cows when I was growing up. One was Betsy Lou and the other was Daisy May."

"Well, now..." I started, ready to make an argument, but not really sure where I was going beyond *Well, now...*

Joe wasn't there for small talk. "What did y'all think of that strange white dude that came through here earlier?"

Jamal looked at Joe, thoroughly confused. He glanced at Evelyn, but she was drawing a blank. He shrugged. "I don't recall seeing no white dude. We were outside gardening most of the day, too."

"You don't remember that lanky drink-a-water that was walking 'round earlier? You yelled at him."

Jamal scratched his head as if to pull a lost memory to the surface. "Maybe. Only guy we saw was spreading a message."

"Jehovah's witness," I said as I nudged Joe's arm. "Told ya that's what he was."

Joe ignored me. "What kind of message?"

Evelyn answered. "Peace. Love. Make the most of everyday. Stuff like that." She then looked at her husband like he was the most handsome thing she'd ever laid eyes on.

Jamal returned her gaze. I swear I saw simultaneous twinkles in their eyes. "That's right. That's what it was for sure."

Evelyn took Jamal's hand. She got up and pulled him toward the front door. "We talked to him too, but he didn't say nothing about that," Joe argued, but they didn't hear a word more.

"Oh, uh, you'll have to excuse us gentlemen. We got something cooking in the oven." Jamal leapt up from his seat and followed Evelyn through their front door. He closed the door behind him. There was an urgency in their movement. A fire that most certainly led to an explosive passion as soon as the door shut.

"Man, they ain't too discreet about it, are they?" I laughed.

"Boy oh boy. Like they a couple of teenagers or something. You'd have to be blind to miss that look she gave him. I guess gardening gets their motor running." Joe was bewildered.

"Attaboy, Jamal. Attaboy," I cheered toward the front door. I doubt they heard me inside, though.

"How'd they mistake that guy for some sort of messenger of love and peace?" Joe muttered the words, like he was talking to himself and not me. He stared at the door a long moment before he finally broke himself from it. "Let's talk to Manny."

We walked on, but Daizy Mae dropped down on the Sheldon's porch and stayed there.

"Suit yourself," I said, a little hurt that she had chosen them over me. "I'll eat these myself then." I popped a little cookie in my mouth.

I was done with my remaining cookies by the time we got to Manny's porch. Joe knocked and Manny answered, beer in hand. He swayed as he talked, eyelids drooping. He mumbled through a similar conversation with Joe that we had with Jamal and Evelyn. Turns out, he didn't remember a strange white man either, but it was easier to believe that he forgot. He was plastered. If there was any doubt he was bombed, it was gone when he called me "Unc." We hardly ever talked, and when we did, he never once called me that, which was fine by me. I never took a shine to calling him part of my family, even if it was through marriage.

Then, the darnest thing happened. He tried to hug me. I pushed him back to arm's length. We weren't about to start that nonsense.

"Go on to bed, son," I advised him as I backed up. "Stay off the sauce for a while."

Joe and I walked back down the street. "Man, that boy's nothing but sorry. Too drunk to remember diddly. And him trying to get all lovey dovey. With me of all people. What you reckon that was about?" I shook my head.

"Jamal and Evelyn are living life to the fullest. Manny is trying to make amends. I guess they've just accepted things." Joe looked over his shoulder at the western sky as he spoke.

"What in the wide world of sports is that supposed to mean?" I asked. "And what're you looking at?" It was still too early for the sunset and the sky was clear.

"Nothing," Joe said. "C'mon. Dinner ought to be ready."

Chapter 26

Joe, Yvette, Felicia, and I sat down together at the table for what turned out to be an out of sight dinner, and not just because of the circumstances. It would have been a dynamite layout under the best of conditions.

Joe was silent, watching Willie, who was in his booster seat at the opposite end of the table. Willie was equally subdued and appeared ever so tired. They were like mirror images of each other, separated by a tabletop and six-plus decades.

Willie's eyes met Joe's, and they held the exchange for a long moment, as if communicating telegraphically. Their faces were stone and their eyes burned with an intensity I hadn't seen either exhibit before that night. Especially Willie. His eyes were full of an enthusiasm that his ailing little body wouldn't allow him to exhibit. I would have never interfered in that moment, but the food was getting cold and maybe Yvette didn't notice their silent interaction like I did.

"Grace, Joe," she said, her hands already folded before her.

Joe snapped out of it and Willie looked down at his own hands, though he couldn't quite get them to hold together like Yvette had taught him. Joe folded his hands and bowed his head, so Felicia and I did as well.

Now, Joe's supper prayers were never long, but they usually thanked the Lord for the food in front of us and the family around him and all the blessings we had gratefully received. On that night, though, his prayer was short and oddly succinct.

"Lord, those were your words in the red letters, so I'm holding you to them. Amen."

With that said, he dropped his hands and looked across at Willie again. Yvette opened one eye and looked at Joe, in disbelief that he was finished. His break from the prayer was enough for me so I went for the biscuits, but I was halted when Yvette continued on his behalf.

"And thank you, Lord, for this food and all the blessings you've heaped upon us. Amen."

"Amen," Felicia and I dutifully recited.

Then, with the unfolding of Yvette's hands, I knew it was okay to dig in. Felicia started making Willie a plate and Yvette grabbed the bowl of beans. Joe leaned back in his chair, still watching his grandson.

"Joe, you alright? You've had your head in the clouds since we sat down," Yvette commented, finally noticing her husband's subdued behavior.

Joe nodded, never taking his eyes off the boy. "Just not feeling quite up to snuff."

"Sounds like what you need is Ol' Red's Rheumatism Medication after dinner," I piped in while I dropped a half rack of ribs on my plate.

Willie seemed as though his mood improved when his momma put a dish of yellow rice in front of him. He plowed into it with reckless abandon.

Joe blinked heavily and slowly, as if breaking his concentration on the boy. When he opened his eyes again, he was looking right at me and finally grinned. "You're probably right."

I was glad to have my bud back, so I kept at it. "In fact, I think I got a little tickle in my throat, too. Might need a preventative dose myself. Can't be too careful with all the crud that's swirling around, ya know?"

That got Yvette involved in the conversation. "As much whiskey as you two drink, I don't see how no germs can survive to make you sick. You pickled through and through like a couple of pigs feet."

"Well, when we're dead, you can just throw us in a jar and put us on a shelf. We'll keep forever," I retaliated, eager to laugh again.

I guess I wasn't the only one ready for a little brevity after the soul-sapping day.

"No way," Felicia chimed in. "When you three old bloods have outlived your usefulness, I'm gonna do like the Eskimos and put you on an iceberg so you can float off into the ocean fog."

"You three?" Yvette trilled. "Felicia! What'd I do?"

Felicia gushed as she laughed. "I might even shoot flaming arrows at the thing so it'll melt quicker!"

"I'll shoot 'em back!" I griped. I held up my hands and mimicked shooting a bow and arrow. I pretended it was a tiny one, just to make it funnier. "Thoink. Thoink. I'll be like Injun Joe out there. How 'bout that?"

"How come every Injun got to be named 'Joe'?" Joe finally joined in.

"Yeah, I'd probably have a good Injun name like Buckskin Bob of the Bugaboo Nation or Walking Hawk Hank of the Hontoon!" I could feel myself starting to roll, but Joe held up his hands in concession.

"Alright, alright," he laughed. "No need to go down that road again."

Yvette guffawed. "You only a walking hawk 'cuz you too full of bull honkey to fly!"

I puffed out my cheeks like I was fat and flapped my arms like feeble wings. Joe laughed.

"Well, saying 'Injuns' is offensive and I didn't say anything about them anyway. I said Eskimos, but if you wanna be Native

Americans, fine. I'll walk you into the woods and leave you for the bears and wolves like they used to do to their decrepit and infirmed." Felicia was getting her wit rolling, too.

"Me and Joe sure to come back with wolf-skin blankets and bear jerky, won't we, Joe?" I snapped back.

"Enough for the whole 'blamed village!" Joe chuckled.

"Felicia said she was leaving me out there too, so when y'all come back, where'll I be?" Yvette said. Her hands were beneath the table, so I assumed they were on her hips since her head was cocked to the side.

"Sorry, ol' girl, we got to bait the traps with something," I said.

"And what are you gonna use for a trap?" she shot back, her head rocking to the other side. "You gonna lay your dentures out open on the ground?" She put the heels of her hands together like a bear trap and snapped them shut sharply. "Those big chompers sure to snap a poor creature in half!"

Yvette and Felicia belly laughed and high-fived across the table while I bit the air near their hands, clanging my teeth, which were indeed partial dentures. Somebody was stomping their feet under the table, but I wasn't sure who it was.

"Might catch a Sasquatch if you're not careful," Felicia belted, tears forming in her eyes.

"Big Foot versus Big Mouth," Joe jabbed, getting the biggest laugh of all. Even Willie giggled at that.

And that set the tone for the next hour. We ate like royalty. We carried on other like we hadn't in a long time. We joked and razzed each other, but only with love and a sincere desire to make each other laugh. Somehow, all the weight on our collective shoulders melted away and we really found some joy, if only for a short time. I am not exaggerating when I say it was the most fun I'd had in ages and the food was better than it had ever been.

The Moore family found each other again in the tempest and pulled into each other and consolidated like a star that contracts into a dense ball of fire and energy, waiting for all the physics to line up and create a supernova that lights the sky for years. I was blessed yet again to be an up-close witness. There, around that table, was an act of God in its purest form.

As for the ribs, Joe had smoked them up just right. Yes, indeed, he smoked those ribs that day. They were out of sight.

Chapter 27

With full bellies that ached from laughing so hard, Joe and I retired to the rockers on the front porch. The night had grown muggy while we ate inside. The air was thick and as hot as a baby's fevered cheeks. A bottle of Old Red's sat on a table between us and we each had a tumbler of that smooth bourbon in hand. Joe stared out into the black western sky. He closed his eyes and breathed deep through his nose.

"Man, you can smell that storm coming, can't you?" Joe said.

I sniffed the air. "All I smell is them ribs still on my lips. Oh, my soul, those were good! What'd you do differently with them tonight?"

Joe kept staring westward, not interested in talking about supper.

"I figure we was so distracted that we didn't fiddle with them in the smoker too much," I continued. "Maybe that's the trick. Leave 'em be and let that smoke soak in over a long time."

Joe snickered at me. "I've been saying that for years. You're the one who is always opening the smoker door and poking the meat and cutting off pieces to sample."

I shrugged. What he said was true. I couldn't deny any of that. Seemed like a good time to change the subject though, and since we were speaking of smoke, I went with it. "I got a couple of stogies over at the house. Bought them last time I went to Daytona. They're short but got a bold kick. I'll be right back."

Joe reached over and put a hand on my leg as I was getting up. "Sit tight. I got something I've been saving for your birthday, but tonight seems like a good night for them."

He stood and shuffled in the front door, so I turned my eyes toward the storm Joe said was coming. I sniffed again. I didn't smell ribs anymore. I had said that as a joke. I didn't smell a storm either. Ol' Joe was always fixated on storms. They worried him to death. Florida nights in the dead of summer was no time to fret about storms. A man could drive himself into a deep depression if he let it bother him too much in the rainy season.

Joe came back out with two long cigars and a lighter. He handed one to me. The cigar was dense and heavy. The leaves were dark and tight. There wasn't a label, but I knew what it was before Joe confirmed it.

"That's a real life Cuban you hold in your hand there, my friend."

I ran the length of it under my nose and inhaled. Boy oh boy, what a rich fragrance it had.

"My goodness. That's nice!" I sniffed again. "A bottle of Ol' Red's and tried and true Cubans. Have we stepped up or what?"

"Only the best from here on out, bubba."

We lit up and took deep draws on the cigars, then we exhaled a cloud of smoke together that hung under the ceiling of the porch like a thunderhead.

"Ho, ho. That's outta sight, baby!"

Joe nodded in agreement as he looked at the smoldering cigar. "Not bad at all."

"We're living the good life, Joe. I wouldn't give this up for nothing, would you?"

"No sir," he said, then he looked off into the yard pensively. I swear to this day his eyes settled on Willie's empty sandbox in the darkness. "Not for just nothing, I promise you that," he added. He looked at me, perhaps wondering if I got the hint. At the time, I didn't.

"Yes sir, brother. Yes sir. We sitting pretty these days." I drew on the cigar again. "This one'll make the book for sure."

"Book?" Joe perked up at that. "What book?"

"I'm thinking of writing one."

"No fooling? What kind?"

"One of a kind, really. I already got the title. In fact, that's where I started with it. The title." I swept my hand across the night, lighting an imaginary marquee in front of me. "'Cigars I Have Smoked'. It'll be all about the cigars I've had over my life. It won't be no magnus opium or nothing. Just a short fifty or sixty-page deal."

"Might get a little repetitive, don't you think? Ain't but so many ways you can talk about smoking a cigar."

"Nah man, ya see, that's what's gonna make it one of a kind. It really ain't about the cigars at all. Each chapter will be about a different one, but the book itself, it'll be about the people I was with at the time. What was happening in my life. Where I was and what I was thinking. I may not have led a book-worthy life, but I've seen some book-worthy things. Met some book-worthy people."

"I'd argue that part about not leading a book-worthy life. You're the most book-worthy guy I've ever known. Ain't many people can say they fought in Vietnam or trekked to the top of Mount Denali or ran a marathon. Shoot, you even threw hands with a kangaroo."

I laughed. All of that was true, but I didn't find it necessarily book-worthy. "I guess I could say I smoked cigars on those adventures and add them to the book."

"Yes sir, you could." He sat for a moment. "Cigars I have smoked, huh?" Joe took a long drag and contemplated my idea. I watched him, awaiting his approval. "That ain't a bad idea," he started. Then, he nodded vigorously and popped in his chair with sudden excitement. "Yeah, that's really good! I like it! Give me some of the stories."

His excitement got me excited. "Well, I figured I'd start with the one I smoked when I went to see BB King in New Orleans. That man can flat out play that guitar! I'd write about that cigar, for sure. Next one I'd write about is the one I had when I was in Old San Juan with Trina. We were walking the back streets between those old buildings. Cool breeze a-blowing in off the sea. Good food cooking. We heard sweet bossa nova music coming out of those open windows."

Now, Joe was watching me. My excitement gave way to something else as I closed my eyes. "Lord, we broke into a dance right there in the middle of the road. You believe that? And when we got back to the hotel, we held each other for so long. So long." I couldn't help the tears that welled in the corners of my eyes right then. I wiped them with my thumb.

"Then, I'd write about that cigar I smoked right by myself on the beach late one night," I went on. "It was a full moon and Trina had just passed on. I rode over to that quiet little area we used to go to and walked in front of the beachfront shops she loved so much. They were all closed, but I just wanted to feel her again."

I lost myself in the memory of that dark time when I had just buried the love of my life and our unborn son. I was wandering aimlessly up the sidewalk and looking through the window of some dark cigar shop. A light flickered inside, which shocked me and made me jump back a step.

The owner was an Italian man about 70 years old. Without a hesitation, he unlocked the front door and stepped out. I was expecting him to scold me for peering through his window so late or to whip out a pistol and threaten to call the cops, but to my surprise, he welcomed me inside.

"I wandered through the humidor as the ol' fella selected a bottle from the wine rack," I told Joe.

At a small table, I sat across from the owner. We each had a wine glass in front of us. The owner sipped his delicately. I did my best to do as he did and not chug it all at once, but it was so good that I wanted to. We smoked his cigars like we'd known each other forever. I talked about Trina and our baby and what plans we had for him and all the things he was gonna be. The old man just listened.

"I spilled my heart out to that fine gentleman. When it was time to leave, he didn't charge me for the cigar or the wine. He did that cross thing with his hands and we said a little prayer for Trina and our boy. I walked the beach for hours after that, just thinking about them. Thinking about her."

I was choked up so much at that point that I could hardly talk. Joe put a hand on my shoulder. "Why didn't you ever re-marry? Nobody would've blamed you if you had."

"Because of that. Because it's called 'remarry'. Any time you re-do anything, it's because it didn't work the first time. Trina and I worked. We worked great."

"That's such a long time to be alone."

"I never felt alone. I've had you. I've had your family. Y'all kept me from feeling lonely. As far as romantic love, well, my ten years with Trina were the best I could have ever hoped for. It was enough to hold me, I guess. I mean, I've had my dalliances since, as you know. Met some nice women, but none that could've taken her place. No sir. To marry any of them wouldn't have been fair. I never could've expected a woman to live a life with me knowing that I was still so in love with Trina. And that's something I don't think I'd be able to hide too well."

Joe nodded. "Besides, when you die, I'm sure you don't want to cross that ol' black river and find Trina standing there with her arms crossed, tapping her toe."

Through new tears, I laughed. Joe did, too. We went on for a while.

Finally, Joe said, "That's gonna be a good book. A real good book. Are you gonna have any chapters about me in there?"

"Oh, you're gonna make it in there for sure," I said, still chuckling. I held up the Cuban. "This cigar right here for starters."

"It'll be nice knowing that my name will make it into print one day."

"Really? You think my book will be published?"

"Sure, it will. It's a solid idea. Beautiful, really. I'm proud of you, bubba."

"Well, then, I'm gonna expand it into a couple of books. First, *'Cigars I Have Smoked'*, then *'Ribs I Have Smoked'*. Think I might even do one called *'Fish I Have Smoked'*. You know you'll be making it in those."

"I smell a franchise."

"When they make 'em into movies, Denzel will play me," I joked.

"Okay. Okay. If I squint at midnight in the fog, I can see it." Joe leaned back into the rocker. "Yes sir. Denzel could do it just fine. Who are you gonna get to play me?"

"That'll be tricky," I started. "Ain't many actors ugly enough. Plus, they're all too tall."

Joe couldn't help but smile and shake his head. "Oh, here we go."

"We might just have to get one of them Muppets to play you," I said.

"Paint Kermit black!" Joe exploded. We stomped and laughed again.

Finally, we fell silent again and I sipped my bourbon and puffed my cigar. Joe looked westward.

"Still smelling rain?" I asked.

"Oh, it's gonna rain alright. A real gulley-washin' toad-choker."

"Pity the poor toads." Right on cue, lightning flickered in the sky. Joe winced a bit. "Hey, man, what was it about that ol' addict today? Why'd he bother you so bad?" Joe sat back and shrugged. "As long as I've known you, I've never seen you scared of nobody," I kept on. "You walk around like you're ten feet tall and bulletproof. Never wanted to tell you that you were barely bigger than a yard gnome 'cuz I didn't want to break your spirit. But somehow, you're the bravest man I've ever met."

"I wish that were true," Joe replied in a low whisper.

"It is true. Besides that guy today, and maybe the occasional thunderstorm, tell me one thing that's ever scared you."

"There's plenty that scares me. Lots of stuff." Joe fell quiet for a moment, perhaps mulling over how to put his oldest thoughts into words. "I'm scared I won't get the chance to teach Willie how to throw a cast net."

I stiffened with bold defiance. "He's gonna be alright, I keep telling you! He's gonna be fine!" My defiance gave way to a low sadness when I paused, then uttered, "He's gotta be."

Joe put his hand on my shoulder again as I hung my head. He was the one in the most pain, and here he was comforting me. It was always his lot to be the rock for others, I suppose.

He started to explain his fears once more. "I'm scared I might get a crick in my neck and not be able to look up at the night sky and see the stars and the moon and the comets." I looked at him then. He was going deep into the well of his soul and I didn't want to miss a word. "Scared I might go to sleep and not dream. That's a waste of eight good hours when I could be walking the Great Wall of China or swimming down to Atlantis or hang-gliding over Alaska right up through the middle of the Northern lights. I'm scared I might read the accounts of Christ's life one too many times. I don't want to ever go through Matthew, Mark,

John, and Luke without shedding a tear. Don't ever want to be so hardened to it that it doesn't break my heart every single time. Scared I might get so down in my back that I can't mow Felicia's yard for her, or lift Willie into my lap, or help Yvette carry in the groceries. Scared I might come up these porch steps one day..."

I remembered the day not too long before when we got home from fishing and were met with a scream from inside his house. We ran in to find Felicia, panic-stricken, bending low on the floor. Yvette ran in from the other room, dialing her phone. Felicia fell aside to reveal Willie on his back in the throes of his first of many major seizures. Joe went to his knees by the boy.

"And find one of my three has gone from me," Joe continued. "If my life is ever empty of one of them, I'm empty, ya hear?" Joe's next words were labored. "But most of all, I'm scared of existing without purpose, living without passion, and dying without cause."

He looked at me, ribbons of tears streaming down his face. I swallowed heavily, trying to stay strong for him for once.

"Dang, Joe. A lot scares you."

He smiled. It was worth a million bucks. "Told you. I'm just a big ol' 'fraidy-cat."

"'Fraidy-cat Joe Moore," I nodded with my own best grin.

When our tears dried up and the laughter died, Joe asked me a simple question. "How'd you survive when Trina and the baby passed? How'd you keep getting up every morning?"

The question stunned me. I had to think about it for a few seconds before I answered. I wanted to say the right thing because I got the sense it was the most important question Joe would ever ask of me.

"I did just that. I opened my eyes and got up. Every morning, I'd see what I could scrounge up for breakfast. Then, I'd go to work and see what that brought along. Day in and day out. The months and years unreeled and piled up on the floor like when a cat starts spinning the toilet tissue on the holder." I looked off and shook my head. "In times like that, you do what you must." I turned to Joe. He was staring at his hands in his lap. "I think that's the secret to life, Joe. We do what we must when we must. Always. That's all we can do anyway."

Joe never looked up from his hands. "Would you have traded places with Trina or the baby if it allowed either of them to live?"

"Yes. Without a doubt, yes. That's an easy one. You would too for Yvette or Felica or Willie."

"I hope so. If the moment ever presented itself, I hope I would."

I waved it off as if what he was saying was absurd. "Of course, you would. And you know why? Because it would be something you must do. See, you and me, we're experts at that. We've both lived our lives that way."

"What if you had to make a pact with Satan himself to save them? Or, even to save just one of them, you had to do that? You had to make a deal with the Devil?" Joe was struggling with something and I could tell it. Suddenly, he was deflated and meek, which was so backwards to his character. For once, he was reaching out to me for help and I knew I couldn't let him down.

"Well," I started, not sure what I was going to say next. But then, from somewhere, the words just flowed. "The Devil can only put you in that position to choose between yourself and your loved one. He'll make sure that situation somehow comes up and he'll test you with it. But he doesn't want you to give up nothing for nobody else. Sacrificing yourself for a loved one is God's work. That pleases Him, not the Devil. I imagine the Devil would be happy as he could be if you did the selfish thing and let your loved one perish at his hands. You die for a loved one, buddy, and you've just made a pact with God."

Joe nodded and smiled a bit, as if what I said made sense to him. Looking back now though, I think I said what he wanted me to say. Not so he could hear it. So I would know why he did what he did later that night.

Joe looked west again. Lightning illuminated the sky like a strobe, but it was too far away for us to hear any thunder. He put down his cigar and bourbon and stood. "Well, if you don't mind, I believe I'll turn in early."

"Headed to the closet?" I quipped.

"No. Not tonight. Yvette's probably going to bed and I'd like to get in there."

I hooted in laughter. "Oh. Okay. You ol' dog. Go on, then. Go on!" Joe grinned. He stuck out his hand and I took it. "Maybe we'll learn some chess tomorrow."

"Willie will be good at chess," Joe said.

"Then we will surely teach Willie." We shook hands for a moment and Joe grinned that megawatt smile down at me. "Good night, Joe," I said.

"Good-bye, my friend," he replied. Joe turned and walked through the front door, leaving me on the porch alone. I puffed the cigar some more. I couldn't shake the feeling that his good-bye had a sad and dreadful finality to it.

Then, like the lightning in the west, something caused my head to clench like a fist. The migraine it brought was immediate. Suddenly, I remembered a verse from Romans that I hadn't read in years, but there it was, pulsing in my mind like it was set to the beat of a battle drum on the plains of Troy.

"If we live, we live to the Lord, and if we die, we die to the Lord. So, whether we live or die, we belong to the Lord."

Now, where in the world did that come from?

Chapter 28

I was in my bed on top of the sheets in my boxers and a tank top, staring up at the spinning ceiling fan. My headache had grown strong by then, but I had loaded up on some Tylenol and was waiting for it to kick in. Lightning flashed through the window and thunder finally followed it, grumbling in the distance a good five or six seconds later.

"*Cigars I Have Smoked*," I whispered upward, dictating my book into the heavens. "Chapter One. While we were smoking a couple of Cubans, I asked my friend, Joe Moore, about the things that scared him. When he first told me, I thought he was just making stuff up. But when I thought about it more, I realized that, for as long as I'd known him, he was only afraid of the most magnificent things."

I stopped when I envisioned some angelic stenographer looking down at me with a frown and a shake of her head. I shrugged up at her and her judgy self. "Well, I never said I was an Eistein-beck."

A bright flash suddenly lit up the room and was followed by a rattling boom. I sat up and looked at the window.

"That was close," I muttered.

Another flash was followed by more angry thunder. Then came the roar of rain. I fell back into the bed as my windows rattled with the arrival of the late evening storm.

All my life, I've lived within an eighth of a mile of the railroad tracks. I got used to the sound a train makes when it passes through. More times than not, a train would go by and I wouldn't even realize it. But if a train ever came down the road right in front of my house, I believe I'd notice. And sure enough, I did. That's what it sounded like. A train. An atomic, super-powered cannon train. Coming right down the middle of Doreen Street.

The streetlight on the power pole in front of Felicia's usually cast a soft white glow against my bedroom window. It blinked out. My digital clock and all the ambient light from electric appliances that usually go unnoticed went off at the same time. In the abject darkness, I went to my window and peeled open the blinds. All I could see was black.

I felt my way out of my room and to my living room window. I looked out to my front yard, deafened by the noise of the locomotive blasting through the neighborhood.

Against the black backdrop of the storm marched the even blacker silhouette of the monster from the West. It skipped up the street, high and thin. Its walls were well-formed and undulating and it carried white and gray debris, like it was bringing home the groceries. It puffed outward, then slimmed back down, then curved at its middle, constantly moving. Constantly changing. The bottom of it spun, making sharp snaps across the street like an upside-down snake, coiling and striking.

That tornado was a jagged thing.

The rain poured down in torrents and blasted against the window like it was a tidal wave coming in from the ocean. Bushes and trees whipped and shredded in the driving wind. The lightning flashed like a strobe light and the thunder boomed relentlessly.

The twister moved up the street toward me like a runaway semi-truck. The pressure change caused a sucking sound around all of the windows and doors in my house. For a second, the outward rush of air through the tiny spaces caused a loud whistle. It was the same whistle I had heard earlier in the day.

Unable to bear the sound, I unlocked the window and pulled it up, causing the air to gush out. Because the lower half of the window was up, the glass was double thick in front of me. Rain washed against it like I was going through a carwash. The lower half of my body was soaked in seconds. I cupped my hands against the open window to get a better look.

The tornado weaved its way down the street, zigzagging from one side to the other, clipping mailboxes and tearing apart houses as it went. Debris flew everywhere. Newspapers, pieces of lumber, shingles from roofs, trash cans.

A red leash, faded to pink by the sun, slammed into the glass in front of me. The upper part of the window, on the outside of the raised lower part, shattered. Had I not opened the window a moment before, the leash would have come through the upper portion of the window and struck me in the face and peppered me with shards of glass.

I dropped to the floor and curled up, screaming at the top of my lungs. It wasn't from the shock of the impact. It was for my poor Daizy Mae. I crawled on all fours from the room, cursing the storm and what it had done to my little friend.

My friends.

My heart sank at the thought of who else was being hurt. Or worse.

Crawling, I made my way to the front door and reached up to turn the knob. It tore from my hand as the door swung outward with a slam. The pressure pulled me out onto the porch. It took all of my power to stand.

At the same time that this was happening to me, Yvette leapt from her bed in her house as the thunder clapped outside and the train sound quaked her windows. She looked for Joe, but he was nowhere to be seen.

"Joe! Joe!" she screamed, so scared and needing him beside her. She ran to the closet with a flashlight in hand, certain that he had taken refuge inside like so many times before. She threw open the door, expecting to see him huddled in a ball on her shoes.

He wasn't there.

On my little porch, I had to grab a support post and wrap my arms around it to keep myself from being pulled into my front yard. The wind howled and the rain flew sideways onto the porch, drenching me. The lightning and thunder only intensified as the tornado marched down the street in front of my house, leaving a wreck of unidentifiable debris in its wake.

I quickly surveyed the street behind it. Trees were down and cars were flipped over. Power lines were ripped and sparking. The danger was everywhere and flying at me.

What am I doing out here. I turned to retreat inside.

That's when I saw the twister make a sudden beeline toward Felicia's house. I knew why I had come out now. I had to do something to save Felicia and Willie. All I could manage, though, was a loud scream at the storm.

Whatever heroism I'd hoped to find within myself was sucked into the middle of that tornado and strewn away like the bits of debris. I began to cry as I stood by helplessly and watched the storm pause in front of Felicia's. It heaved and flexed, gaining strength.

Right then, through the violence, I saw the front door of Joe's house burst open. The top hinge gave away, tilting the door outward. Joe ran onto the porch in his boxers and undershirt. Like me, he was pulled toward the storm. He was able to stop himself at his porch's railing. The rocking chairs slid towards him as the tornado broadened its shoulders and whipped its tail. Without hesitating, Joe leapt off the porch and stumbled across his yard, right toward it.

The tornado lurched at Joe as if it saw him coming, and snapped at him from the bottom. It was warning him away. To better make its point, it snatched one of the rockers (Joe's, not mine) off the porch. The chair soared toward him. He stopped as it was ripped to pieces right in front of him and devoured by the twister.

Joe fought the sucking wind as he went to Felicia's house. He made his way around Felicia's car parked sideways in her front yard. He climbed the steps to her porch, opened the front door, and disappeared inside.

The tornado puffed out in anger and attacked the power pole next to the sidewalk. The fierce winds struck a loud whistle once more as the roar of the storm intensified yet again. It gnashed its jaws around the pole and splintered it at ground level with a jarring crack. The pole tilted, then fell toward Felicia's house. Sparks and fire circled inside the walls of the storm. The pole smashed down across the top of Felicia's roof, right over Willie's room. There was a loud boom from the impact. More sparks danced across the roof as it collapsed under the weight of the pole.

The roof ignited in flames and the whole side of the house tumbled in on itself. As the pole drove downward, deeper into the top of the house, the base of it smashed across the hood of Felicia's car.

I left my porch and stumbled toward her house. The fierce wind kicked me to my knees. By then, the flames engulfed the house. I felt the wind pushing me down, like an elephant was stomping on my back. It took every bit of strength I had to keep from collapsing to my chest in the mud.

The tornado turned from the shattered pole and began wavering across Doreen in the direction of the empty field with the large oak, just as Joe blasted out of Felicia's front door. He was holding Willie in his arms, cradling him.

Joe held his grandson close and carried him down Felicia's porch steps and out into the yard, desperate for shelter.

Finally, as the twister moved away, I was able to get to my feet. From the middle of my yard, I waved both hands overhead. "Joe! Joe! Over here! Bring him here!"

Joe saw me hailing him and started for me, though the downed power pole was between us. He went toward the pole, which was only a couple of feet off the ground between Felicia's car and her crumbled house. I got to the middle of it before him and waited, motioning for Willie. Poor Willie was wailing with fright.

"Bring him here!" I yelled. "My house is safe!"

Behind us, Felicia exited her burning house as Yvette rushed from hers. They saw me and Joe and Willie in Felicia's yard at the middle of the pole.

As they saw us, so did the tornado.

It paused in the street as its shoulders bulged outward. Above the shoulders, its head turned, spinning all the way around. Like an owl.

Joe saw it. He darted for me on the other side of the downed pole. The loud gushing of wind gave way to a shrieking whistle again. The tornado doubled back at breakneck speed.

Joe was still a few feet from me when he screamed, "He's after Willie!"

With the tornado charging back at him, Joe turned to Felicia's car only two yards away. I didn't even have time to consider how in the world a tornado could be a 'he' or target a specific person.

The car's hood was crushed under the weight of the pole, which caused the back tires to be jacked nearly off the ground. Joe dashed to the car as the tornado raced for him. He held Willie with one arm and opened the back door. The car seat was strapped inside and he put the screaming boy in it. He whipped the restraint over his head and buckled it between Willie's legs, just as the twister coiled up off the ground, whipped its tail back and forth, then struck downward and burrowed into the top. In a second, the entire car was buried in the belly of the furious funnel.

I was yanked hard into the pole in front of me. It was like a giant had swung a tree trunk and plowed it into my waist. I lost my air and flipped over the pole to Joe's side of it. Breathless and in pain, I landed on my back in the pooling water.

In the same instant that I smacked my back on the ground, I saw the winds lash around Joe. Still in the open door, he gripped the frame of the car along the roof. The wind was unmerciful and the roar was deafening.

Then, I finally heard it. The storm spoke in the gushing, hissing voice of the day's jagged stranger. "Mine."

Joe yelled with defiance into the vortex. "No!"

It screeched even louder as if in reply, then it grabbed Joe's ankles and lifted his feet over his head. He held tight to the car. It shook and rattled but remained anchored by the downed pole. Its metal frame bent in the middle. Willie cried.

Joe's fingers began to lose their grip. He looked past his feet, deep into the churning, sucking chaos above him. After a moment, it took him.

Joe Moore disappeared into the maelstrom.

Chapter 29

The tornado stretched into a skinny, crooked swirl of black as it danced across the yard and back toward Doreen Street. Its distinct walls began to fade, and its strong winds diminished and dwindled.

I struggled to my feet and rushed for the car. Willie was still screaming, and he was much more audible without the wind in my ears. I reached in and unbuckled him and pulled him into my arms.

I looked at the retreating cyclone, perhaps wondering for a moment if it would see that Willie was still alive and return again with a vengeance. In the end, I knew it wouldn't. If it had truly been after Willie when it came, and was truly denied, then it had gotten a fair trade in return and was satisfied.

The trauma was too much for Willie and he passed out in my embrace as I ran toward Felicia, who was crossing her front yard. The conflagration that was her smashed house illuminated the whole neighborhood. The heat from it boiled and evaporated the rain over it before it even hit the ground.

Yvette rushed by me, toward the car where Joe had been taken from us, but I stopped her with an outstretched arm. The puddles were deep around it and I wasn't sure if the electricity from the downed pole coursed through it. Felicia was screaming when she took Willie. I turned to Yvette and embraced her. She saw what happened. I didn't have to tell her. She howled into my chest.

I looked over her head at the tornado. It was barely discernible as it neared the old oak tree in the field. There was victory in the way it strutted. The tree's limbs shook in the wind for a moment. And then, there by the lone oak, the twister vanished.

The lightning and thunder and rain remained, but the beast was gone.

Felicia came back to us. Willie was catatonic. Felicia held him up to me, crying. I pulled her in, too. We huddled close together, drenched and sobbing as a group. I tried to stay strong for them, but all I could do was take Felicia's phone from her and call 911.

Chapter 30

In the distance, beyond the vacant lot and the lone oak, flashing red and blue lights from police cars, ambulances, and firetrucks pulsed across Joe's house as they approached our neighborhood from the other side.

Destruction marred the length of the street, but somehow, some houses were miraculously untouched. Doreen street flooded with our neighbors as they filed out of their houses. They watched and helped with the rescue effort as best they could amidst the scattered debris and wreckage.

By then, the fire at Felicia's was dying, but it drew the initial attention of the first responders. EMTs took Willie to their ambulance. They tended to him with great care. Within minutes, with Felicia by his side in the back, the ambulance whisked him away.

She gave no thought to her home, which was a total loss. She cared only for her little boy.

The hours ticked away. Sunlight broke on a new day. By then, there were more cop cars and firetrucks. There were TV vans and helicopters and power company trucks, and hundreds of people combing our street, digging us out of the wreckage.

Do I even have to say what else those crews found?

The roof of Manny's house was opened up like the top of an aluminum can. Manny's body was found embedded in the hood of his newly waxed car.

Ida Macon's home was caved in. She stood in her nightgown in front of her demolished home. She cried on a neighbor's shoulder for hours.

The Haynes's place was swept away, as if by a whiskbroom. Only the foundation and some anchored timbers remained. How they survived is impossible to figure.

The Sheldon's block home was reduced to a pile of rubble. Jamal and Evelyn didn't make it out. They were found in their bed, locked in a loving embrace. Their house had collapsed around them, but a bedside lamp still stood, its lampshade not even tilted in the slightest.

Felicia's house was a mound of smoldering charcoal. And Joe's was fine except for the single hinge that was torn from the front screen door. In fact, it didn't lose nary a paint chip.

But it lost so much more.

With no time to spare, Willie was transported from the local hospital to Dr. Dawkins's facility by helicopter. Yvette made the several hour drive there to be with Felicia during his emergency surgery. Someone had to stay behind to keep an ear out for Joe. I did that part.

And I wandered.

I found a framed picture of Joe, Yvette, Felicia and Willie that was in Felicia's front lawn amidst the debris. The glass was cracked.

I collected Daizy Mae's leash from under my window and wrapped it around my hand and wrist so tight it cut off my circulation.

I was approached by a TV crew, but refused their request for an interview.

When things began to settle down by mid-morning, I replaced the hinge on the tilted screen door at the Moore's house.

By the afternoon, two bulldozers worked their way up and down Doreen, cleaning the broken pieces of our neighborhood.

The power company had fixed all the downed power lines and had moved on to surrounding, less-affected streets. Fire investigators sifted through Felicia's ashes.

And several streets over, a lineman in a cherry-picker ascended to the top of a tree to cut away branches that had fallen onto a line.

I'd like to say that Joe was found safe and sound. After all, God is capable of such miracles. He parted the Red Sea and brought Elijah to Heaven in a fiery chariot. He even stopped time itself.

I still like to imagine that a lineman found Joe there, kicked back on a branch like he was sitting in his rocker, holding a cigar in the gap of his missing front tooth, smiling. When he spoke, the cigar didn't jostle a bit.

"Good to see you fella, I was starting to get hungry. What a ride that was!"

I guess there are physical laws that even God can't or won't overturn. Like the most elementary one: What goes up must come down.

Joe's body was found in that tree by the lineman. There was no more life in him. He had been carried three blocks away. Only a deceitful, spiteful, horribly evil force could eject a grown man so far.

I drove the two hours to the facility to tell Yvette myself. I held her for a long time while she cried. Felicia took the news better than I expected. She was too worried about Willie, who was still in surgery with Dr. Dawkins.

It took four days and that many trips back and forth between the hospital and my home before I finally caught Felicia accepting her father's fate. I walked in the hospital room. She was there alone, curled up in a rocker recliner, knees drawn to her chest. To her bosom, she clutched the picture I had found in her yard.

She cried over and over, "Oh Daddy. Why? Why?"

I stood by her with my hand on her shoulder. Then, the door swung open. Willie was in a little wheelchair being pushed by Dr. Dawkins. A nurse followed. The boy was holding a cookie and grinning wide. His hair was shaved, and a stapled wound was visible on the side of his bald head.

"Good news," Dr. Dawkins announced. "The scan is negative and..." He saw Felicia and didn't interrupt the moment any further.

But Willie didn't notice his mother's dismay and anguish. He was too busy enjoying his cookie. He held it up toward me, offering me a bite. His smile was worth a million bucks.

Then, I knew why.

Chapter 31

We had a fine graveside funeral service for Joe at a cemetery shaded by sweeping oak trees that wasn't too far from Doreen Street. There were over a hundred people and just as many flower arrangements.

Dr. Dawkins and I were the front pallbearers. Bill was behind me. We carried Joe's casket toward the open grave while Felicia sang a hymn so beautifully that everyone wept. Willie was walking by that time. He didn't need the wheelchair anymore. His stance was strong while he stood by Yvette. He didn't waver a smidge.

It was a proper funeral, I guess, but I figured a better send-off, at least one more fitting for Joe, would have involved some smoked mullet, robust cigars, and a big bottle of bourbon. Funerals are for the living, though, and not necessarily the deceased. Drift too far from tradition and those left behind feel as though they've cheated or dishonored the departed.

We lowered his casket into the grave. People dropped flowers on top of the casket as they walked by the open hole and paid their final respects. I stayed until everyone else was gone and two men from the funeral parlor cleaned up the seats and tent from the area around the grave. When they left, another man began shoveling dirt on the flowers and the casket. I asked him if I could take over. He shrugged and tossed me the shovel, plenty eager to let me do that job for him in the heat of the day.

When I finally finished, I had taken a lot longer than he would've and he was a little bent out of shape that I was cutting into his afternoon. I was sweaty and my nice shirt and tie were dirty. Thankfully, I'd removed the onliest suit jacket I had to my name, so it stayed clean. I'd quite literally buried my life-long best friend and something about that seemed poetic and right. Some part of me was satisfied. I hoped Joe would be satisfied, too.

Then, from the gentle rustle of the leaves in the trees around me, I heard Joe sigh. "This kind of formality isn't us," he rasped in a low whisper. "You can do better than this for me." I knew when I heard him that he was right. I could do better for him.

"Would it have been too much trouble to say something before I grabbed the shovel," I whispered in a soft, hushed tone so only the trees could hear.

The gravedigger fellow looked at me like I was crazy. "What'd you mean, ol' timer? You wanted it!"

So much for my whisper voice.

Chapter 32

It was Christmas time before I could finally bring myself to give Joe a memorial I figured he would enjoy. I sat on my newly expanded porch in the surviving rocker from Joe's. It didn't seem proper to go and sit at Yvette's house without Joe being there, so I had added onto my porch. It was covered and big enough to accompany the rocker.

I hadn't made too big of a fuss about it. There was only a single, overhead bulb lighting the porch. No fan like at Joe's. I had every intention of making my porch bigger and screening it in and whatnot, but all that could wait for a time when I had more energy.

A scratchy Louis Armstrong holiday track played softly over the little radio that I had set up next to my chair. I lit a Churchill (my first since Joe died), then sipped some Ol' Red's bourbon from a tumbler. A cool breeze blew through and rustled my shirt. It felt good.

I looked down the length of Doreen. In the five or so months since the tornado struck, the neighborhood had recovered. Christmas lights adorned many of the houses up and down the street. We were ready for a joyous season.

I thought about Joe for a long while.

Then I thought about my book. *Cigars I Have Smoked*. Catchy title, but the last chapter would be my masterstroke. I'd call it *The Cigars I Have Smoked With My Friend Joe*. It would be the longest chapter and in it I would write about Joe Moore and who he was and what he did for his grandson.

It is within a tornado's nature to tear things apart. It is its brutal purpose. Joe pulled those he loved together with an equally determined ferocity. Somewhere along that chapter, I would give a portrait of a mighty shepherd of men who fulfilled his own destiny in defiance of a savage storm. And he saved his family from an unbearable loss twice in the same day.

I would also explain what Joe did for Isaac. I would relay how Dr. Dawkins was a new sensation in the medical community and had started to be referred to as 'world renowned neurosurgeon Doctor Isaac Dawkins' because he had developed a new way of operating on a horrible brain condition that had so far been inoperable. With his revolutionary new technique, he'd already saved fifteen dying children like Willie. In just five months. In the coming years, he would personally save hundreds. His technique would be perfected and used world-wide. If my math was correct, I figured millions more would live because of him. And that meant Joe was right again.

With all of that said in the monumental last chapter, if I had time, I'd fix the problems between the races with some of Joe's witticisms. A nod and smile to each other. Start there and build up. All interpersonal relationships that have ever succeeded have had their genesis right there. It really was that simple. We've known it forever. It's a shame that every few years we have to repackage and relearn it.

Other people, not me of course, but other people would probably go on to say that Joe's chapter was the greatest bit of writing in American literary history.

Every man wants to leave his name written on the world somewhere when he dies. Long after I was gone, people would talk about my little book about cigars, especially the end of it. *The Cigars I Have Smoked With My Friend Joe* would be my imprint on history. I finally had my lasting legacy.

Yep, I was rocking in my chair and right proud of the book I had yet to start and the praise the world would surely heap on me because of it. Ol' Louie was singing his heart out and everything was right again.

That's when I saw a light flick on at Yvette's house. The blinds parted and I saw a dark, tiny silhouette peering out of the window. Since Felicia's house was gone and only a cleared lot remained, I could see Yvette's house perfectly. The light was only on for a second, then it went out. I rocked in the chair and puffed the cigar. I followed that with a sip of bourbon. I looked back at Yvette's. Still dark.

Then, I heard a creak as Yvette's front door opened. I made a mental note to oil it the next day. When I heard it rattle shut, I checked my watch.

Awfully late for someone to be up and wandering, I thought.

Within the soft radius of light from the new streetlamp on the new power pole between our houses, the tiny silhouette appeared on her porch. I watched it walk out on the porch and down the steps. The little shadow didn't take the sidewalk but scurried across the empty lot that separated us. The patter of quick steps on damp grass grew close. I leaned way forward in my rocker to watch. The little silhouette was gone from the streetamp's radius of light until it appeared in the much smaller, dimmer illumination provided by my little porch's bulb.

Willie stood at the bottom of the two steps leading up to my porch, dressed in a T-shirt and undershorts. His hair had grown back. He held a plastic cup in one hand and a Slim Jim sausage in the other. He smiled up at me.

"Hey, little man," I said. "What're you doing awake?"

"I heard your music."

"Yeah? You like it?" Willie nodded.

"Can't beat ol' Pops," I affirmed. "C'mon on up here." He climbed the steps and stopped in front of my rocker. "Does your momma know you're out here?" The boy shook his head. "She's probably fast asleep, ain't she? Grammy, too, I reckon."

He nodded again, so I took a drag on the cigar and sipped the bourbon. Willie mimicked me perfectly, putting the sausage between his lips, then taking a sip from his cup.

Well, that just made me laugh.

"What're you doing anyhow?" he asked.

"I'm just sitting here thinking about the ending of my dang book."

"What dang book?"

"Oh, just this little deal I'm gonna write."

"Like 'Cat in the Hat'? I got that one. Uncle Isaac gave it to me."

"No, probably not as good as that." I sipped from the tumbler. When I looked back, Willie was holding the sausage between his fingers just like I was holding the cigar. The cup rested in his palm like the tumbler was in mine. And there he stood, looking up at me. Way up at me, like I was on a mountain. I couldn't help but laugh again as the universe opened up and revealed itself.

I dropped my cigar in the tumbler. It went out with a fizz in the liquor. I put the tumbler and the doused cigar on the small table beside me. I wouldn't touch either ever again. At least not while he was watching.

"What's so funny?" Willie asked in his sweet little voice. "It just came to me, my last chapter. My really real last chapter. It'll be all about my legacy. It's gonna be outta sight!"

"Outta sight!" Willie repeated.

I guess he didn't know I was talking about him. Why in the wide world would he? I grabbed him under his arms and lifted him to my lap. He rested his head on my chest.

"You figure I might get a piece of that sausage?"

Willie handed the sausage to me, so I tore it in half. I gave one part of it back to him and put the other in my mouth, like a cigar. We started rocking in the chair.

"Have you ever been fishing with a cast net?" I asked, knowing that he hadn't.

"Nope."

"Nope? Don't say 'nope'. You gotta use proper English. That street talk will make you sound like an uneducated varmint. And don't forget to use your manners. Now try again. Have you ever been fishing?"

"No sir."

"Attaboy. So how 'bout I take you tomorrow morning?"

"Yes sir!" He was eager, I'll give him that.

"I'll come get you bright and early and we'll go out and catch a mess. I'll show you how to cook 'em in that smoker out back of Grammy's. How's that sound?"

"Outta sight!"

"And I got you a chess set for Christmas, but maybe we'll get it out early and learn to play. Would you like that?"

The boy nodded vigorously.

I ruffled his hair. "You best go on to bed then. I'm gonna be over there to get you before you know it."

His vivaciousness turned to sudden anxiety. He shook his head against my chest.

"What's the matter?" I asked.

"I can't go back to my room! There's a monster in my closet!" He was scared just that fast. I felt his little body start to tremble against mine.

"A monster? There's no such thing as monsters. It's probably just a shirt sleeve or something sticking out. Now if we're gonna be fishing partners I can't have you afraid of silly things."

"But it's real! You should see it!"

I nodded. "Okay. Fine. Let's go have a look. I'll show you there ain't, I mean, isn't any reason to be scared."

"You won't be scared! You're probably not scared of anything!"

"Sure I am."

With that, I took Willie in my arms and stood up. I carried him down my steps to the sidewalk. We started slowly toward his house. He nestled his head against my chest, getting comfortable.

"I'm scared I might get a pinched nerve in my neck and I might not be able to look up at the night sky. I'm scared I won't be able to see the moon and stars and all those comets, all so bright and pretty. Heck, I'm scared I might go to sleep and not dream. That's a waste of eight good hours when I could be walking the Great Wall over there in China and climbing the pyramids in Egypt or swimming down to Atlantis. I'm scared I'll read them Bible stories about Jesus one too many times..."

And so, for the next few minutes, I told him all the magnificent things that scared me.

Jeff Malphurs is a Respiratory Therapist from New Smyrna Beach, Florida. When he isn't writing or working, he enjoys spending time with his wife, Angie, and their two daughters, Zoe and Jillian. Jeff has also written a young adult book titled *Santa Claus Rebooted & Revamped.*